BOOK TWEN

CAN BARNABAS STOP QUENTIN FROM BRINGING HIS COVEN TO COLLINWOOD?

Quentin Collins' coven of witches, centered in the Castle Asariana in Venice, was the scandal of the city. Reports of the bizarre practices of the Devil worshipers, all of whom were beautiful girls, circulated widely, and invitations to the parties that Quentin sometimes held to attract new members to his cult, were greedily coveted.

Then two Americans died while spending an evening at the castle, but before the authorities could investigate, Quentin and his entire group vanished. Soon after, Quentin showed up at Collinwood, with the intent of establishing his cult there.

Barnabas knew it was up to him to stop Quentin before Collinwood was turned into a center of Black Magic and Satan worship. But who wielded the stronger power—Barnabas, or the Devil himself?

Hermes Press

Originally published 1970
This edition ©2021 Curtis Holdings, LLC. All rights reserved.

Published by Hermes Press, an imprint of
Herman and Geer Communications, Inc.

Daniel Herman, Publisher
Troy Musguire, Production Manager
Eileen Sabrina Herman, Managing Editor
Alissa Fisher, Graphic Design
Kandice Hartner, Senior Editor

2100 Wilmington Road
Neshannock, Pennsylvania 16105
(724) 652-0511
www.HermesPress.com; info@hermespress.com

Book design by Eileen Sabrina Herman
First printing, 2021

LCCN applied for: 10 9 8 7 6 5 4 3 2 1 0
ISBN 978-1-61345-238-7
OCR and text editing by H + G Media and Eileen Sabrina Herman
Proof reading by Eileen Sabrina Herman and Sara Dena

From Dan, Louise, Sabrina, and Jacob for Karen Fowler

Acknowledgments: This book would not be possible without the help and encouragement of Jim Pierson and Curtis Holdings

Printed in Canada

Barnabas, Quentin and the Witch's Curse
by Marilyn Ross

CONTENTS

CHAPTER 1

A nita Burgess would always associate that August of 1900 in Venice with the overwhelming sweet fragrance of hundreds of cut roses, the hot winds blown across from the Libyan desert, and the stench of the side canals of that ancient maritime city which reeked with pollution. It was here during a series of suffocating days and nights that she was to meet Quentin Collins and be caught up in a train of weird and evil events that would take her back to her native United States and the Maine estate known as Collinwood!

It was in that Venice of long ago that she first entered the Castle Asariana, a palace with a three-story ivory marble facade elaborately ornamented with columns and balustraded windows. The great mansion rose out of the sickly greenish water of the canal. And it was within this castle that the rich American expatriate Quentin Collins had set up a headquarters of a cult devoted to black magic which had become the scandal of this city of scandals!

It was said that Quentin Collins truly possessed the evil eye, that his Black Masses to the Devil were the homage duly paid by a servant to his master. It was common gossip that the coterie of young women from many parts of the world who had joined him in the mansion as followers of his cult were the loveliest in the city of a hundred and fifty canals.

On the Rialto Bridge spanning the Grand Canal, before St. Mark's Cathedral with its five beautiful domes, or by the Palace of the Doges with its open-air promenade, the luscious beauties of Quentin's cult could be seen in their black gowns and veils. The natives pointed them out and the tourists stared at them. Despite their severe black garb they were outstandingly lovely.

It was in the Castle Asariana that Quentin first invited Anita to become one of the maidens of his group. He showed her through the great palace with its tapestries, inlaid marble, gold decoration and elegant furnishings. It was there also that she had first noted his obsession with roses. All through the many fine rooms, roses were set out in vases, bowls and jars of every sort. The odor of the delicate pink flowers permeated the house. And with a sly smile on his side-whiskered, attractive young face he had told her of one of his favorite historical characters.

He had been showing her his fine collection of paintings. One of these was the "Roses of Heliogabulus" by an English painter named Sir Laurence Alma-Tadema. It depicted Heliogabulus, most decadent of all the Roman emperors, who began his rule in A.D. 218. A priest of the Syrian sun-god, he dressed in flowing robes, painted his cheeks red and, until his assassination, reigned in a most corrupt manner. The painting depicted an orgy in which the participants were smothered to death in a cascade of rose petals. It showed the lovely women of the court gradually being overwhelmed by the thousands of petals descending on them in a low, enclosed area. Eventually they smothered to death amid the fragrant petals. It was revealing to watch the look of satisfaction on Quentin's face as he told the story of the colorful painting. As they moved on, Anita had given a tiny shudder, thinking that he would probably enjoy condemning his own lovely followers to a similar fate if the mood suited him.

But this was later, after she'd gotten to know him well. Her first meeting with him had been a brief one at the mansion of another expatriate American millionaire living in Venice. Anita and her brother, Jeffrey, on a grand tour of the continent, were attending an afternoon party as guests. Quentin was there holding court and acting in a generally superior way. His eyes had showed a brief gleam of interest when Anita had been presented to him. But he had made no attempt to open a conversation with her. Instead he'd turned to some others and continued a harangue about the quality of Venetian silver.

A few days later a messenger came to the hotel where she and her brother were guests and delivered an invitation from the brash young man. Standing in the old-fashioned elegance of their living room in the hotel suite, she'd read the letter to her brother. It was a hot and humid day. The sun was streaming in through the tall windows. Anita was a small dark girl with her hair rolled in buns at either side of her head. Not really pretty, she still had good even features with large, attractive dark gray eyes.

She was wearing a flowing green dress with a low cut neckline and she held the letter for her brother to see. "Would you and your brother do me the honor of attending a masquerade ball at the Castle Asariana this evening at ten," the invitation read.

Jeffrey, her brother, was twenty-four, a year younger than Anita. He lolled impatiently in an exquisite crimson-upholstered easy chair. His leg swung indolently over one arm of the chair and the rest of his body was slumped in it. He was small like Anita and handsome in the same restrained way. He was wearing a suit of gray woolen material much too heavy for the hot day and his temper reflected his too warm condition.

Frowning, he said, "It's the last place I have any desire to go!" He had curly black hair which he wore long over his collar.

Anita put down the invitation with a reproving glance for her brother. "But why?" she asked. "We have no engagement for tonight."

"What difference can that make?" Jeffrey demanded. "Surely you've heard of his shady reputation?"

"He seemed very handsome and dignified at the party the other afternoon," she said in Quentin's defense. "And he is an American like us."

"More disgrace to Americans," Jeffrey said with a scowl. He brushed a spot of dust from his broad blue cravat and went on. "Don't tell me you wish to join that harem he's collected!"

She blushed and folded the note. "I haven't thought about Quentin Collins as a person at all. He is an American living here and holding a party. He's asked us to attend and I can't think of any good reason for us not wanting to go."

Jeffrey snapped, "Because the man's a shady character."

"Come now," she reproved him. "He's accepted almost everywhere in the city."

"As a curiosity. An evil specimen who people enjoy meeting so they can gossip about him later."

"Really!" she pouted.

"This rotten heat isn't enough," her brother complained. "We have to have an argument over something like this." He rose angrily from the brocade upholstered chair. "You can't tell what will happen if we go to his house."

"It's to be a masquerade party. Isn't that innocent

enough?"

"Not the sort he's liable to hold," Jeffrey warned her. "It could turn out to be a wild orgy. This Quentin Collins is an evil man!"

She smiled resignedly. "You never will get over your narrow-mindedness. Just because Quentin Collins lives a different sort of life you are quick to condemn him. I see him as a perfectly ordinary young man from Maine with more money than he knows what to do with, enjoying the stir his actions have caused. I'm sure he acts the role of Devil's disciple merely to get attention."

Jeffrey gave her a sarcastic glance. "Next you'll be telling me he's a fine young man."

"He probably is," she said.

He was about to give her a prompt reply but a knock on the door of the suite interrupted him. He went to open it and let in Arnold Term. Arnold was a pleasant young banker, also from Philadelphia, who was traveling with them. He was engaged to Anita, so she was glad to see him because he usually took her side in any argument between her and Jeffrey.

Jeffrey showed the young man in the room, saying, "You're just in time to find your wife-to-be engaging in an unreasonable argument!"

Anita went to Arnold with a smile on her pretty face. "That's not so, at all!"

The blond young man touched his lips to her cheek and took her hand, saying, "I'm sure it isn't. And I intend to marry you no matter how black Jeffrey paints you."

"Noble of you!" Jeffrey declared in disgust. "But you might be well-advised to listen to my warnings." He pointed at her. "There is a miss who can get you into who knows what sort of trouble."

"What is it now?" Arnold wanted to know.

"It's a lot of nonsense!" she protested.

Jeffrey, who'd been pacing up and down before the window, turned to them. "It's nonsense all right. But not in the way she means. Our charming Anita has received an invitation to attend one of Quentin Collins' parties and she wants to go!"

"We were both invited," she pointed out. "And Arnold as well."

Jeffrey came toward her and with a determined glance took the letter from her hand. He quickly scanned it "As I thought! It has no mention of Arnold."

The young banker smiled good-naturedly. "That makes no difference. You two can go without me. I'll find something to do."

"No," Anita said, turning to him. "If we attend the party

we'll all go. I'm sure that Quentin Collins meant to include you in the invitation. Your name not being on it is merely an oversight."

Jeffrey eyed her sarcastically. "He meant to exclude Arnold. He has an interest in you. He doesn't want your husband-to-be around to interfere!"

"That's your evil imagination!" she told her brother.

Arnold smiled at her. "Do you really want to attend the party?"

Anita hesitated. In the beginning it hadn't been too important to her. But now that her brother had made so many objections she felt she should assert herself and insist on going. Had she guessed what this would lead to, she would never had taken such a stand. But the results of her decision were not to be revealed until later.

She spoke in a hurt tone. "I think I should be allowed to do something of my own choice. Ever since we began this tour of Europe, Jeffrey has made all the decisions as to what we should and shouldn't include. It's terribly frustrating!"

"Terribly frustrating!" Jeffrey mimicked her. And he told Arnold, "You two should have waited until your honeymoon and made this trip on your own. A lot of thanks I've gotten for all the arrangements I've made. All the work I've done to make the tour a success!"

Arnold smiled. "That's precisely why I wanted the three of us to do this before the wedding," he said, "I value you as a guide. And I'm sure Anita does too. But maybe she is right in this. It's a small thing. Why don't we all find suitable costumes and attend the fellow's party? We'll be leaving Venice in a few days, anyway. And you should enjoy yourself. From all that I hear Quentin Collins is always surrounded by a host of pretty girls. There'll surely be one for you."

Jeffrey stood before him frowning. "I think of more than the opportunity of meeting a pretty girl. I'm concerned about possible danger for Anita. They claim that fellow places women under a spell. I have an idea he wants to add her to his cult of demon worshipers. And I have no wish to see my sister a devotee of the Black Mass."

"You're exaggerating terribly," she complained. "I'll be with Arnold. What harm can come to me?"

"Wait and perhaps you'll find out," was her brother's dramatic reply.

But she didn't pay any attention to it, for she knew she'd won the argument. She quickly left the two young men and set out in a gondola to the home of the friend who had given the party at which she met Quentin Collins. The daughter of the house was about her own age and named Dorothy. She was at home when Anita stepped from the gondola onto the terrace in front of the proud mansion. Within a few moments Anita was shown into the presence of the young woman by an elderly servant.

Dorothy Carr was delighted to hear of Anita's invitation to the party as she was also going. "Of course I have costumes for you, your brother and Arnold," the young woman said. "I'll have them sent over within the hour."

Anita smiled at the diminutive, titian-haired girl. "Jeffrey did not want me to attend the party. You know how difficult brothers can be!"

"I have never had one," Dorothy said. "But I can imagine. My father can be very domineering when he likes. But he is allowing me to attend Quentin's masquerade."

"Is Quentin really as evil as people try to say?"

Dorothy hesitated. "I wonder that myself. None of the girls who have joined his cult and live there will tell what goes on in the palace. But I know they all are forced to do hard work to keep the place clean and in order. There are some assigned to the kitchens and they prepare all the food for affairs like the one this evening. They are devoted and close-mouthed. He seems to have some magnetism that makes them willing to surrender their freedom to him."

"The evil eye, perhaps?"

The other girl looked solemn. "I have heard that he is a devil worshiper. And that regularly the Black Mass is said there. The young women are spoken of as a coven of witches. But a lot of it stems from jealousy. From people he offends or doesn't invite to his parties. He is very headstrong in such matters and will tolerate no one he doesn't like."

"That is a rule most of us would like to follow," Anita suggested.

Her friend smiled faintly. "I can see that you are taken with Quentin. Already you are strongly in his favor."

She blushed. "Not at all. I was only introduced to him. We barely exchanged a greeting."

"That can be enough with Quentin," Dorothy warned her. "Your brother could be right. You are engaged to marry. It would be unfortunate if Quentin should come between you and Arnold."

"No chance of that. Arnold is very understanding."

"Still, Quentin is a strange, sly person," her friend said. "There was one girl who left her fiance to be with him. Apparently he didn't encourage her to join his cult, or she discovered something about it of which she didn't approve. A few weeks later her body was found in one of the canals."

Anita frowned. "But should Quentin be blamed for that? It could have been the girl's fault."

"The gossips say he was to blame. That he broke her heart and then would have nothing to do with her." Dorothy hesitated and then lowered her voice as if she wanted to make sure no one would overhear her. "The most scandalous of all the tales about him is that he is a werewolf!"

"A werewolf?"

The other girl nodded. "Yes. They say that under a full moon when the Sabbath of the Witches has been held, they form a ring around him. Then he puts on a belt made of wolfs hide and makes an incantation to the devil. In a twinkling he changes shape from man to wolf!"

"That's too incredible!" Anita protested.

Her friend sighed. "Of course I have never believed it. But there are people here in Venice who claim they have seen a wolf outside his castle on moonlit nights."

"They don't care what they say as long as they scandalize him," Anita complained.

"There is truth in what you say," her friend agreed. "But if Quentin gets you to himself tonight, take care."

"I will," she said.

She returned to the hotel in a rebellious state of mind. She felt it was mean and cruel of the social world of the ancient city to libel the attractive young man from Maine. She would not believe any of the ugly things said about him until they were proved true to her.

The costumes arrived later in the afternoon, complete with black masks for all three of them. She had a gorgeous gown of pale blue with a white cape of three-quarter length and a narrow black mask to disguise her identity without hiding her beauty. A black outfit with knee breeches and black cape had been provided for Arnold, along with a broad-brimmed hat to complete the garb of an eighteenth century gentleman. Jeffrey had been assigned the brown robes and rope belt of a friar along with a bald pate wig to complete his transformation from youth to age.

As darkness came they all gathered in the living room of the hotel suite to compare their costumes under the soft lamplight. Already they looked like the dwellers of an earlier and more colorful age.

From behind his mask Arnold said, "I think this is going to be an exciting evening!"

"Perhaps too exciting!" Jeffrey, as the aged friar, said dourly.

Anita laughed as she linked her arm in Arnold's and said,

"He sounds as ancient and vinegary as he looks!"

Arnold laughed with her and then asked, "Isn't it time for us to leave?"

"It is," she agreed. "And Dorothy told me he wants at least two flaming torches to be held in each gondola. So there will be a galaxy of them as we approach the entrance to Castle Asariana."

"That sounds like some Satanist rite to me," her brother said darkly. "I don't think we should take part in it."

"Nonsense!" Arnold said. "I think it will make the canal surrounding the castle glow with light. From the landing the guests' costumes will be revealed in all their colorful design. It would be ill-mannered not to comply."

"I agree," Anita said.

Jeffrey, in his brown robes and bald wig, looked strangely different. "I can see that I'm going to be outnumbered in every argument," he snapped.

So when they had the hotel steward get them a gondola they also had him provide the torches. As they began their short gondola ride up the canal to the palace where the party was being held, Arnold lit the torches. He held one aloft and Jeffrey reluctantly took the other. Anita watched ahead eagerly for signs of other guests on their way to the party.

It was not long before they converged on the smooth, oily waters of the canal with several other gondolas containing masked and costumed guests bearing their lighted torches. As Quentin had predicted, the area at the landing before the imposing three-story palace became as bright as day. The historic canal seemed alive with the small craft as they passed crumbling stucco houses with geranium-filled balconies, and motionless trees rising from dank smelling, walled-in gardens. At last they reached the Castle Asariana.

They had to wait their turn to disembark from the gondola. It was a spectacle to see the illuminated rooms of the distinguished building casting shimmering yellow reflections on the dark water and the array of gondolas with masked guests holding torches aloft. Lanterns glowed from both sides of the marble archway over the entrance.

Anita was caught up in the magic of it all. Bantering and laughter filled the air, and then Arnold was helping her up onto the landing with Jeffrey following. They took their places in the reception line.

Inside, the heavy fragrance of roses filled the air. The flowers were everywhere, set out in great bunches in priceless vases. Quentin Collins received his guests alone. He wore an eighteenth century costume of brown and gold velvet with white stockings and wig. He wore his mask, but it did not disguise his good-looking face. And his black side whiskers peeked out impertinently from under the wig.

When he took Anita's hand he let her know he recognized her. In a warm voice he said, "My one hope for this evening was that you should be here."

"Thank you," she said with gentle amusement.

"I shall expect to dance with you," he added. "And I have some things I'd like to discuss with you. I've been away from the United States so long I feel like a foreigner. You will be able to bring me up-to-date."

"I'll try," she promised.

She moved on to be joined by Jeffrey and Arnold. Jeffrey was still in a suspicious and nagging mood. "What did he take all that time to say to you?" he asked her.

Anita sighed. "He was just being the pleasant host!"

"He took plenty of time about it," Jeffrey grumbled.

Arnold gave him a reproving glance. "If anyone ought to complain it is I. And you're hearing nothing. I say, let us mingle and enjoy the party."

From an upper level the strains of the orchestra could be heard. They went up the broad marble stairway to the ballroom. On the way she glanced about her at the damask chambers with dark oak beams. The hallway of the second level had branched glass chandeliers, crimson plush walls and a frescoed ceiling of a shapely goddess studying herself in a looking-glass. Through wide doors was the ballroom. Great paintings adorned its dark marble walls and it was crowded with costumed couples dancing.

She uttered an exclamation of delight. "It's fantastic! I'm so glad we came."

In his black gentleman's outfit Arnold looked regal and imposing. He smiled at her from behind his mask. "I agree," he said. "We may never see a party such as this again."

Jeffrey was still in a bleak mood as he stared gloomily at the dancers. "There is evil behind all this," he assured them.

"Dear Jeffrey! How wonderful you look! I think you should take priestly vows and dress like that all the time!" It was Dorothy Carr, in a Pierrette's gay yellow and blue checked costume, who had come up to them. She at once grasped Anita's brother by the hand and drew him off towards the dance floor.

As Anita watched her friend and Jeffrey join in the dancing she smiled at Arnold. "Thank goodness for that!"

"Dorothy knows how to handle him," Arnold said. "She should silence his complaints."

And so it turned out. They were relieved of Jeffrey's dismal comments for the balance of the party, while he, caught up in the activity, seemed to be actually enjoying himself. Anita danced with Arnold for quite a while and then they began walking through the different rooms off the second floor hallway and admiring them.

It was while they were doing this that Quentin Collins came to join them. He seemed in a jovial mood and he was escorting a dark, lovely girl whom he introduced as Mara Caprizio.

Anita at once asked her if she was also a visitor to Venice. The dark girl replied in a slightly accented voice, "No. I live here in the palace."

So she was one of Quentin's cult. Anita felt she should have known this. The girl's striking beauty of face and figure were evident even in mask and costume. But it was her eyes that fascinated Anita. The girl had an almost hypnotic gleam. And they were strange in color, having the near amber shade such as is common in cat's eyes. Those eyes gave Anita a strange feeling.

Quentin was smiling at her. "I've been promising myself a chat with you. I consider this the ideal opportunity."

She hesitated, all Jeffrey's warnings now beginning to come back to her. She said, "I really should go back to the ballroom. Arnold hates to miss any of the dancing."

"Then Arnold shall not miss any of it," Quentin said at once, and turning to Mara Caprizio, he said, "Take that young man into the ballroom and let him discover that your dancing matches your beauty."

The dark, tall girl smiled at Arnold. To Anita's surprise he returned the smile, hardly glancing her way at all. He seemed enchanted with this member of Quentin's cult. When she extended a dainty hand to him he took it and guided her towards the ballroom entrance without even excusing himself. It struck Anita that he was behaving like someone in a trance.

"Your gentleman friend appears to approve of Mara," Quentin said quietly as he stood at her side watching the two join the dancing couples.

"Yes," she said, slightly agitated but not wanting to show it.

"Mara has great charm," Quentin said, "so the time will go by swiftly for him. Meanwhile we can have our chat."

Nervously she said, "Really, I don't think we have anything to talk about."

Quentin was persuasive. "Don't you believe that," he said. "Let me show you more of the castle."

Before she realized what was happening he had guided her through a narrow door at the end of the hallway and into a room of incredible splendor. Golden mosaics shone from the ceiling, jeweled screens lined the walls and at the far end of the room was a raised platform draped in black, in contrast with the opulence of the rest of the room. And on the black-draped table there rested a grinning skull with dark eye sockets. Seeing it staring at her, she gave an involuntary gasp of ahum.

Quentin Collins had removed his mask and was smiling at her. "You mustn't be alarmed. It will do you no harm. The skull plays a part in the ceremonies we hold in this room."

She felt a small panic rising in her. "I'd rather not hear about what goes on here," she said.

But the good-looking young man had much too strong a will to be put off by this. He held onto her arm and deliberately urged her farther into the room until they were standing just before the altar and the skull.

"It is to remind us of the swift passage of life and beauty," he said in a low, odd voice.

"I find it out of place in such rich surroundings," she said, trying to avoid the skull and giving her attention to the colorful frescoes on the room's ceiling showing young women disporting themselves by a garden pool.

"But that is why it is here. We must think of the harsh reality of life as well as enjoy ourselves," Quentin said. "You have met Mara and seen how lovely she is. Yet one day she will be reduced to a skull like that set out here."

She gave him a look of revulsion. "What a dreadful thought on a night supposedly being devoted to pleasure."

His hypnotic eyes met hers. "You surely don't mind my revealing some of the secrets of our manner of living here?"

Anita tried to avoid his eyes but couldn't. They fascinated her; they bored into hers, and seemed to somehow paralyze her thoughts. She felt her resentment and opposition to him melt away. She wanted to react only in a way that would please him.

He was staring at her now, very serious in manner. "You are lovely enough to become one of our group," he said in that low hypnotic voice. "I want you to think about it. I need you here. Forget about that young man you're engaged to. And forget about returning to America. Stay here with us."

"I don't know," she said, faltering.

"While I am here as leader you have nothing to fear," he intoned in a mystical way. "You will be safe."

She swallowed hard and whispered, "Let us go back to the others."

He nodded. "In a moment. But first I want to help you conquer your fear."

He guided her close to the platform and gently took her

hand and brought it close to the skull. Then he pressed her fingers on the smooth, cold surface of the shining bony head. She should have screamed out her fear. But under his spell she didn't. Not even when she watched with horrified eyes as a large ugly spider appeared on the skull near her hand and began crawling closer to it on ugly, hairy legs!

CHAPTER 2

Just as the spider reached her hand Quentin released his hold on her and she was able to quickly draw away from the skull. She was weak and trembling from the mental strain of those terrifying minutes, and yet she didn't resent the attractive young man's actions as she should. It was part of the strange spell he'd cast over her.

Studying her with a sardonic smile, he said, "I'm sorry if I seemed needlessly cruel, but I wanted you to understand."

She didn't know what it was he wanted her to understand. She was too completely confused. And yet she was willing to accept what he said. It was as if she were two people, one Anita Burgess, the observer, watching coolly from the outside, and the other Anita Burgess, the compliant, willing to endure anything he asked of her.

She looked up at him, sensing that he was enjoying the power he held over her. She said, "Why did you bring me in here?"

"To introduce you to our ritual chamber," he said. "You'll be returning, I'm sure. We are making great discoveries here. Dredging our minds for new knowledge of our secret selves. And you shall join us. Be one of us."

She shook her head. "I don't think so."

"Return when the house is not filled with guests," he said. "Then we can discuss it properly."

Anita wanted to refuse. But there was that strange power in

him that she couldn't seem to resist. She said weakly, "Let us go back to the others."

His eyes met hers very directly. "By all means," he said. "And you'll forget all about your little scare in here, won't you?"

She stared into those strange eyes. "Yes," she said in a low whisper.

They were out in the crowded hallway again and she felt much better. All that had taken place in the other room was blurred in her mind. She remembered having been given a tour of the house. And that was all that was clear in her mind.

The orchestra was still playing and many dancers remained on the floor. Masks had been removed but the colorful costumes lent an air of gaiety to the evening. Now liveried footmen were serving food from a table stacked with all varieties of succulent treats. It was a fitting climax to the exciting ball.

Quentin remained at her side, nodding and speaking pleasantly to his guests as they passed. Then he took her onto the dance floor. She waltzed with him and for the moment forgot everything else in the pleasure of the lively dance. Then they were with Arnold and Mara once again. The four of them stood near the entrance to the ballroom and engaged in small talk.

She saw that the tall, dark Mara was as strikingly lovely as she'd supposed now that she'd removed her mask. She had perfect features and a warm smile. And those odd amber eyes were not so strange when they blended with her face. It was the black mask that had made them stand out. The girl seemed to have struck up a warm friendship with Arnold. The blond young man acted as fascinated with her as ever.

Quentin smiled at them and said, "I have a suggestion. Since we have all become such good friends I'd like you both to have dinner with Mara and me tomorrow evening."

Arnold gave her an inquiring glance. "I'd enjoy it. What do you say, Anita?"

She wanted to refuse. Deep within her was a nagging fear, but she surprised herself by saying quietly, "Whatever you like."

Mara gave Arnold one of her intoxicating smiles. "Then it is settled," she said. "You'll both be coming."

"I suppose so," Arnold said.

"You will find it much more appealing here when we have some privacy," Quentin said. "I'll send a gondola to your hotel for you at seven thirty."

"That is very good of you," Arnold said, seeming afflicted by the same confusion Anita recognized in herself.

Quentin bowed to them. "I must leave you now. Some of my guests are beginning to go and I must say goodnight to them."

He gave Anita a parting smile and then he and Mara walked off in the direction of the stairway. Anita turned to look at Arnold and found her fiance seeming rather embarrassed.

"I didn't intend to neglect you," he apologized. "But that Mara is an amazing girl. The time seemed to pass very quickly with her."

"It didn't matter," she said quietly. "Quentin was showing me through the house."

The blond young man was staring at her. "You look pale. It's very hot and it's been a trying evening. Would you like to leave?"

She nodded. "I think so, if you can find Jeffrey."

"I'll go look for him," Arnold volunteered. Then he hesitated a moment and rather awkwardly said, "It might be wise if we didn't mention tomorrow night to him."

"Yes," she said. "That struck me too."

"He'd never approve of us coming here even though it is perfectly all right. To save a lot of argument I'll say I'm taking you to one of the restaurants."

"That would be a good idea."

"Jeffrey never need know the difference and there won't be any fuss," Arnold said with a quick smile. Then he left to search for her brother.

It was strange that Arnold should have had the same thought she did. And it was the ideal solution to a difficult problem. What Jeffrey didn't know wouldn't hurt him. They'd have their evening with Quentin at the castle and her brother would be none the wiser.

She stood there alone for quite a few minutes before Arnold returned with Jeffrey. For a change her brother seemed in good spirits. He smiled at her and said, "The night didn't turn out so badly after all. Dorothy Carr can be a lot of fun."

"I'm sure of it," Anita said, and the three of them prepared to leave together.

That night Anita had a series of nightmares. In them she was back at the Castle Asariana. She was alone in that room with the jeweled screens and the frescoes on the ceiling. The skull on its black-draped table spoke to her in a harsh voice, inviting her to stand before it. Then, as she drew near it trembling, the macabre thing upbraided her in a scornful manner, so that she woke in a sweat.

Still, she didn't dare confide any of this to Jeffrey. She and her fiance had made an agreement to accept Quentin's invitation and say nothing. She knew it was taking a chance and perhaps wrong; she also vaguely remembered something unpleasant happened there the previous night, but aside from her dream she retained no clear knowledge of it. She began to suspect that both Quentin and Mara were exercising some strange form of hypnotism over both her and Arnold.

In the afternoon she went for a walk and met Dorothy Carr before the five arched doorways of the Cathedral of St. Mark. There beneath the gilded horses on the terrace they stood in the busy square talking.

Dorothy eyed her knowingly. "You spent a great deal of time with Quentin Collins last night," she said.

She heard this with some uneasiness. "Why do you say that?"

"I saw you go off with him and it seemed a long while until you returned. I didn't mention it before Jeffrey because I know how prejudiced he is about Quentin."

"He's most unfair."

Dorothy showed some concern. "Still, he may not be all that wrong. Quentin is a complex character. I wouldn't like to see you hurt by him."

"I won't be," she said confidently.

"I still would be careful," was Dorothy's advice. "It seemed to me that Quentin was looking very pleased with himself when he returned with you last night."

Anita didn't want to talk about it. She said, "I think you imagined that."

"Perhaps," Dorothy said with doubt clear in her tone. "And that beauty, Mara, one of his collection of girls, surely went out of her way to charm your fiance. Arnold seemed to be blind to everyone in the room but her."

"He found her very pleasant," she admitted.

"No doubt Quentin carefully instructed her," was Dorothy's dry comment. "I think those girls in his black magic circle obey him to the letter. So just you and Arnold take care."

Anita managed a smile. "We're not children and I'm sure Quentin is much less dangerous than gossip around here maintains."

The other girl sighed. "I don't know. That enormous party last night started tongues wagging again. They wonder where he gets the money to spend and entertain so lavishly. They hint the Devil is generous to his disciples."

"What an awful thing to say!"

Dorothy gave her a meaningful look. "Things do go on behind the golden door of that palace," she said. "Things that are only whispered about."

"Vile gossip!"

"No," Dorothy said. "There's so much smoke there has to be at least some fire. A few months ago Quentin had a cousin visit him here. A charming man named Barnabas Collins. He only remained a few nights and then vanished mysteriously with his manservant."

"What is the point of that?"

"They claim this Barnabas didn't approve of what he found taking place in the castle and so wouldn't remain. As I've mentioned, he was very gentlemanly and nice."

"I can't believe his not staying as Quentin's guest had anything to do with Quentin's behavior," she said. "There probably was a sound reason for his leaving. He may not have intended to remain more than a short time."

"He told several people he planned to spend at least a month in Venice," Dorothy maintained.

"I don't know anything about it," she said.

"Nor do I. But there must have been something. So for the rest of your stay here I'd keep my distance from Quentin if I were you."

"Thank you," Anita said quietly. Then she excused herself and left her friend as quickly as she could.

Evening found her changing into an orange silk dress she considered her best. When Jeffrey remarked on her elaborate preparations she told him Arnold was taking her to dinner at a famous restaurant.

Jeffrey showed interest. "Why didn't you invite me along?" he asked. "I get sick of the food here at the hotel."

Her cheeks burned as she hastened to say, "There are times when Arnold and I enjoy privacy."

"Indeed?" Her brother lifted his eyebrows. "For two romantics, you didn't spend much time together at the party last night. You were with Quentin much of the evening and Arnold always seemed to be dancing with that lovely dark girl."

"You're exaggerating," she reproved.

"Not much," her brother said. And he frowned. "I've heard some other gossip about that Quentin Collins today and I must say the general opinion is that he's a very corrupt young man."

"I don't think you should harp on that," she said. "We're only spending a short time in Venice, not living here. How can it matter to us what he is?"

"True," Jeffrey admitted. "I just wanted to warn you in case he tried to see you again."

She picked up her fan, shawl and evening bag from the table in the hallway and told her brother, "I don't want to keep Arnold waiting so I think I'll go down to the lobby and meet him."

"Are you sure he's not still in his room?" Jeffrey asked.

"He said he'd meet me downstairs," she replied. She then left hastily before her brother could question her any further. Jeffrey was clever and with a few more questions he'd have her confessing that they were actually going to dinner at the Castle Asariana. And then there would really be an argument.

She stood uneasily in the lobby of the hotel until Arnold came down. She thought he looked nervous and guilty also. He came over to her at once.

"I'm glad you came down," he said. "I wasn't looking forward to going to the suite and being questioned by Jeffrey."

She smiled faintly. "That's the reason I decided I'd better meet you here."

He looked relieved. "The gondola Quentin sent is outside waiting." He hesitated. "You're sure you want to go? You don't think we're making a mistake?"

Again there was that inner conflict. She knew she should have said they were taking a risk. That it might be better not to go. But the other part of her calmly took charge and she heard herself saying, "I'm sure we'll have an interesting evening."

"Then we may as well get on our way," Arnold said. The canal was not nearly so busy as on the previous night. In the distance they could see the lights of several large boats in the harbor. They sat in silence as the gondolier used his single oar to speed the one-sided craft towards the distant lights of the palace of strange rumors.

But the lights of the three-story marble-front building were much subdued from the previous night. Inside the castle there was a soft yellow glow from the windows at the second level. And the two outside lamps cast their rays faintly on the landing. They left the gondola and mounted the circular marble steps.

Before they could knock, the door was opened by one of the liveried footmen. Then an older servant met them inside and showed them to the rear of the building. There in a large room lit only by candles on the dining table Quentin and Mara were waiting for them.

"You're exactly on time," Quentin said, coming to her and taking her hand and touching it to his lips. He was dressed in evening clothes, and Mara, at his side and smiling, wore a close-fitting black gown of shining sequins.

Arnold and Mara seemed to only have eyes for each other just as on the night before. Quentin talked easily of the party and other unimportant things. He insisted on having wine before dinner and a servant came with glasses on a tray and served them. Anita took her glass of the ruby liquid and at the same time paid some attention to the room.

The candles gave so little light it was hard to pick out many details. But she saw that the ceiling was enormously high and there were huge, colorful tapestries hung around what appeared to be gray stone walls. The near darkness gave the big room an eerie atmosphere.

They sat down to dinner with Quentin next to her. Mara and Arnold were at the other side of the candlelit table. The meal began with a delicate fish course and was as fabulous as the food of the previous night. As they ate, Quentin spoke grandly of the Venice of medieval days.

"That was when I would have liked to have lived here," he said, smiling at her. "It was one of the great cities in those days. One of the really important places. The tall palaces crowded all the way to the waterfront, those were the fine buildings by which we recognize Venice. The Campanile, brick-red and genial. The Palace of the Doges, gorgeous but severe. The Basilica, domed and glittering. Rags fly everywhere, bells ring all through the day, great crowds fill the Piazza and surge down to the docks. All is movement, color and dazzle. In the glass factories, the furnaces blaze, giant skeletons of ships lie in the shipyards and in the street of the Frezzeria, the bowmakers shape their bows. A city alive and vibrant!"

"You make it seem so," Anita said, impressed.

"I'm infatuated with that long-ago Venice of silk merchants and financiers manipulating their currencies," he said with a sigh as the flame of the candles cast a romantic light on his fine profile.

"Don't you care for the Venice of 1900?" she asked. "It is the only one I've known, so I'm thrilled by it."

Quentin smiled and touched a hand on hers. "It will do for us," he said, those hypnotic eyes exerting their power again.

She tried to avoid them and turned to her plate. She said, "I hear you had a cousin visiting you. A Barnabas Collins."

"Who told you that?" His tone was suddenly changed and harsh.

She said, "Dorothy."

"I see," he said. "What else did she tell you?"

"She said he was very nice."

"Indeed? Nothing more?" His tone was icy cold.

Nervously she looked at him again. "She mentioned that he planned to stay a long while and then left very suddenly."

The good-looking face of Quentin Collins showed a twisted smile. "I suppose Dorothy wondered about that?"

"Yes. I guess so."

"Barnabas is an eccentric. He never carries through his plans. He became restless after a few days here and left without even bidding me goodbye. He's a most ungrateful type."

"I see," she said quietly. But she felt he was lying to her.

The explanation had come from him much too glibly. There was something annoying in his assumption that she was simple enough to be taken in by the story.

In that cutting tone, he asked, "What other gossip did you hear about me?"

She sat back from the table and nervously gazed across it to see that Mara and Arnold were so engaged in an intimate conversation they were not even listening to them. She sighed and turned to Quentin.

"Nothing that I can recall at the moment." It was not the truth but as close to it as she dared venture.

The young man was looking at her sternly. "I know there are ugly stories going the rounds about me."

"Oh?"

"And I'm positive you must have heard some of them," he said.

"People will gossip," she said quietly.

"Especially about things they don't understand," Quentin shot back. "And I refuse to allow anyone to know about my private affairs. The great steps in research that I am directing here."

She didn't know what to answer, so rather lamely she said, "Perhaps that is best."

He smiled cynically. "They would like to drive me away from here. But they won't succeed. They are jealous of my talents."

"That often happens."

Quentin's expression was derisive, and she expected that she was included in the derision. "If you listen long enough you will even hear it said that I have the ability to change myself into the shape of a wolf. That I am a werewolf. I promise you, the gossips have outdone themselves."

She was finding the conversation difficult and thinking that her brother had been right. Coming to visit Quentin again had been a bad mistake. She was beginning to suspect that not only was he a hypnotist of ability, but a madman as well!

From across the table Arnold spoke up, "Mara wants to show me some of the fine sculptures on the rear balcony. Will you excuse us for a little?"

Anita felt a growing terror as she saw the two get up from the table and knew she was going to be left alone with the weird Quentin in that great dark tomb of a room. Before she could voice any protest Arnold and the exotic Mara were already leaving the room. They disappeared through a door she hadn't noticed before.

She turned to Quentin and saw there was a mocking smile on his face. He said, "You look frightened. Are you?"

Anita faltered. "This room is overpowering. So gloomy."

He laughed curtly and got to his feet to refill his glass with more wine. He brought the bottle over to her glass and saw that she hadn't touched her wine yet.

"What's the matter, doesn't it suit you?" he asked. "It's a vintage brand. Best in the cellar!"

"I haven't felt like it," she said.

He downed the glass of wine and then looked at her with that taunting expression on his face again. "You're really terrified of me, aren't you?"

She tried to hide her fear. "No. I wouldn't say that."

He leaned a hand on the table and brought his face down close to hers. "But I would! Dorothy told you a lot more about me than you admitted!"

"No!" She was so tense she almost shouted it.

He straightened up so that he loomed above her in the dark shadows of the big room. His face was distorted with anger. "I know what they say. That I came to this palace and caused the death of the old man who took me in as an honored guest. Am I to be held responsible because he was tired of life and took poison? Because he left me this place, am I to be pointed out as his murderer? Do you call that fair?"

Her hands were clenched and she fought to keep calm. "No, of course not," she said, humoring him.

His eyes burned into hers. "Those gossips are crucifying me with their lies! Talking about my black magic cult! Sneering at the girls who have come here and are so devoted to me and the cause! Do you stop to think of the cause?"

She shook her head. "I don't know about it."

He paid no attention to her. He was off on a harangue for his own satisfaction. A release from his own pent-up anger. "We are doing a great work here. Black magic can be a science, a very exact science. One day it may rule the world! And what better place to begin than here?"

Anita said nothing. She eyed the door and hoped that Arnold and Mara would soon return.

Quentin was intoxicated by his own words as much as by the wine. With a sweeping gesture, he said, "We have a perfect headquarters here. And a faithful group to build on. You can be one of us, Anita. You are welcome to join us!"

"I'm being married," she protested.

"To him?" he asked with scorn, indicating where Arnold had been sitting.

"Yes."

"He's not worthy of you," Quentin told her, those eyes fixing on hers again. "You see how Mara twists him around her finger!"

"That means nothing," she said. "He likes her company."

Quentin smiled cruelly. "Do you believe he really cares for you?"

"Yes."

"And you'd sacrifice the glory I can give you here for marriage with him?"

"Yes," she said, rising. "I don't want to talk about it anymore. Let's join Arnold and Mara."

Quentin blocked her from moving towards the door. "Just one moment," he said, staring at her with those menacing eyes. "Let me tell you a few things."

She was frantic now. "I don't want to listen!" she protested.

He reached out and took her arm roughly. "But you will!" he said. "Let me prove to you what a weakling this man you claim to love is. Let me tell you about the girl he's found so interesting."

"It's not important!"

"I think it is," Quentin gloated. "You must have heard of our Black Masses here? The offerings to the Devil? You saw the jeweled chamber last night and your fingers touched the skull!"

She was near tears. "I can't remember anything!"

"Because I didn't wish you to," he said in his suave way. "But now I'm telling you about it all. Mara is one of my flock. One of those dedicated to his Satanic Majesty!"

"I don't care!"

"You will when you hear more," he said. "You see her as a beauty and so does your husband-to-be. But does he guess the risk he is taking now in being alone with her? Does he guess that she is a monster?"

She gazed at his burning eyes. "You're mad!"

"Don't believe it," he said. "Do you know what a Gorgon is?"

"No!"

"Mara is a Gorgon! A killer of men! A daughter of Medusa!"

"Stop your ravings and let me go," she begged him. His fingers were like steel and his grip on her arm had never relaxed.

"I'll let you go in good time," he said. "But first you must listen to me!"

She could see that he had worked himself into a sadistic, raving state. There could be no reasoning with him. Brokenly, she said, "Go on."

"You see Mara as a lovely young girl!"

"Yes."

"But she bears a curse! A curse that brought her to be one of my coven of witches. They all bear the mark in one way or another or they wouldn't be here. In spite of their youth and beauty they are criminals or suffer some sort of curse! I need a priestess, pure and untainted! That is why I want you to join me!"

"Please!" She begged him to let her go.

"Mara came to me bearing the curse of Medusa," he went on. "She is a Gorgon. And when the moment comes that lovely face of hers changes into a mutilated and distorted horror! A face so ugly that to look at it brings death itself!"

"No!" she protested, certain now he was mad.

"Any man who sees that horror of a face is struck dead," Quentin gloated. "That is Mara's secret!"

"I don't want to hear anything else," she said, half-moaning.

He stared at her and slowly a change came over him. Some of the fanatical rage drained from his good-looking face. He gazed down at her with the burning eyes holding a blank expression.

In a stunned voice, he said, "I'm sorry. I was carried away in my anger. I didn't mean to behave as I did."

She saw the passing of the fit of madness from him and felt a bleak ray of hope. "My arm," she said pitifully. "You've been hurting me."

He looked surprised and at once let her go. "I didn't mean to do that," he apologized.

"Where are the others?" she asked.

He hesitated and then said, "At the rear of the palace. On the balcony. We can take the stairway."

She was turning to head for the door when from a distance there came a woman's eerie scream. A scream so bloodcurdling that it froze Anita for a moment. She had never heard anything so terrible!

CHAPTER 3

She turned to Quentin with horror shadowing her pretty face. He was standing a few feet from her looking vaguely concerned. The scream had barely faded when it came again. As frightening as it had been before. A kind of banshee wailing!

In a whisper, she asked Quentin, "What is that?"

"I don't know," he said. "It's out back!" And he hurried by her on his way to investigate the eerie cries.

She followed him, not daring to guess what they might be about to discover. Quentin rushed ahead of her down a short corridor that led to the open and the foot of a high, sheer flight of marble steps. Slumped in a heap at the bottom of the steep steps was Arnold.

It was Anita's turn to cry out. Pushing to his side she bent down to examine his motionless form. His head was bleeding and grievously injured to the eye. She could note no sign of life.

Quentin was on the other side of him. After a few seconds he lifted his eyes to hers and said solemnly, "He's dead."

"He can't be!" she protested.

"No hint of breathing," Quentin said, rising and turning to stare up at the head of the steep marble steps. Still standing there in a kind of spell was the dark and lovely Mara.

Anita rose with tears in her eyes. "She did it! She killed him!

You made her do it!"

Quentin eyed her angrily. "Don't be a little fool!" he snapped. "He fell. It's as simple as that. He somehow lost his footing and fell. Steps as steep as these often cause accidents."

"No!" she protested. "Look at her! She's standing there shocked by what she did."

Quentin murmured, "The curse of Medusa!" And then he started up the sheer flight of steps to Mara, who hadn't moved. Anita hesitated, reluctant to leave Arnold, but then her desire to prove her contentions about Mara overcame her and she followed Quentin up the steps.

When they reached Mara she was standing rigidly, a hand clasped to the railing, eyes staring straight ahead in horror. Quentin called out her name and received no sign of attention from her. With an oath he reached out and slapped her hard on either cheek. It had the desired result. Mara gave him a startled look and then collapsed sobbing in his arms.

"What happened?" he asked her.

"Stumbled," Mara gasped between her sobs. "We were on the way back."

"He couldn't have!" Anita said. "Arnold wouldn't have stumbled! It had to be you!"

Mara raised her head and looked at her despairingly. "No!"

Quentin glanced at Anita angrily. "Don't try to question her now. She's in no fit state!"

"She knows what happened well enough," she accused him. "And so do you." She stared at the crumpled body at the foot of the steep stairs again and her eyes blurred over once more.

"We can't argue about that now," he said. "I'll take her in to one of the other girls." And he left supporting a still sobbing Mara.

She stood there alone on the open stairway that faced on a canal. Her eyes again wandered to the inert body of Arnold far below. Guilty feelings crowded in on her. She blamed herself for what had happened. She had been the one to insist on going to the party and that had resulted in tonight's visit and his death. She was sure in her mind that Mara must have somehow caused him to make the fatal plunge down the stairs.

It occurred to her that the weird wailing cries of the girl had not brought any of the other members of the cult to the scene, not even any of the servants. It was as if all the dwellers in the eerie old palace were aware that some diabolical plot was under way and had been instructed not to interfere. Horror and guilt fought for control of her mind as she stood there on the balcony.

The police should be summoned, she realized vaguely, but she didn't know how to go about that.

Then Quentin Collins appeared again looking distraught. He said, "I managed to get her to her room. She's in a bad state."

"The police," she said, staring at him. "They must be told."

He nodded. "I've left word with one of the servants to do that." He glanced down the steep stairs to the huddled body of Arnold stretched out at the bottom. A look of revulsion crossed his pale face. "This is no place for you to be. Come with me." He took her by the arm and guided her inside through the door.

It brought them to the ornately decorated hallway that led to the ballroom. It was empty of people in contrast to the previous night, and she was awed by the strange silence of the old mansion.

"We'll go downstairs," he said.

They went down the broad marble stairway at the front of the house which the guests had used the night of the party. These stairs were wide and not steep. Compared to them the back steps were dangerous.

Anita was silent, grieved and stunned by Arnold's fatal accident. When they reached the main floor he took her to the living room and sat her down in a high-backed chair. Then he brought her a silver glass of some bitter liquid which had a red color.

"Drink that," he told her. "It will help you."

She accepted the drink and sipped from it gingerly. It did help her after a few minutes. As she came out of shock she was conscious of all sorts of things that should be done, such as notifying her brother of what had happened.

She glanced up at Quentin, who had taken a stand near her. "Jeffrey must be informed," she said.

"Yes. Don't worry about it," Quentin said gazing down at her with those strange, overpowering eyes.

"He didn't know we had come here," she faltered.

"Oh?"

"We were supposed to have gone to a restaurant. He will be surprised and angry when he learns the truth," she worried on.

The young man with the dark side whiskers regarded her ironically. "There is little he can do about it now."

She stared up at him forlornly. "To have this happen so far from home. We were all three enjoying the tour of Europe so. Why did Mara have to do such a terrible thing?"

Quentin frowned at her. "You must stop insisting that Mara killed your fiance. It just isn't so!"

"But she must have! You were there when we arrived at the scene of the accident."

"That was what it had to be," he said quickly. "An accident! Mara is no murderess."

"Then she must be mad!" Anita exclaimed unhappily.

"Earlier you told me some weird story about her. Of how her features changed at certain times and she became horrible-looking."

He nodded. "She suffers from the Gorgon curse. Her beauty changes in a few seconds to a hideous mask of disfigurement. A face so distorted that some are said to die of shock on seeing her. You will remember the legend of Medusa, the hair of twisted serpents and the face that struck men dead?"

She sat forward in her chair and told him dramatically. "Mara caused Arnold to die. And it was not by any Gorgon curse. I'm sure it was deliberate!"

He glared at her through narrowed eyes. "Why would she do such a thing?"

"You must know that better than anyone else," she said defiantly. "You had the girl here under your spell. She was your follower."

Quentin looked discomfited. "You're going by the gossip now. Because she chooses to live here and help with my experiments for the betterment of humanity doesn't mean she is my slave. I'm not responsible for her actions."

"I've seen what goes on here," Anita said. "And so I find your story hard to believe."

Quentin sat down by her, impulsively taking her hand. "Don't let this tragedy come between us," he said. "You'll always regret it if you do."

She stared at him in horror and drew her hand from his. "I know you can't be trusted," she told him. "I remember how you acted in the dining room before the accident. You behaved like a madman and hurt my arm!"

"Because I'm so in love with you," he said earnestly. "You are the type of person I need to help me here. I couldn't bear to think of you going away. Don't let Arnold Tenn's death influence you. Remain here and be my wife and chief priestess. There is important work to be done!"

His look of fanaticism as he spoke frightened her. She shook her head. "I could never marry you or remain here."

"You needn't be afraid," he said hastily. "I can make what happened tonight seem natural enough. No one will question that your fiance died in an ordinary accident." The more he said the more he revealed his villainy and increased her fear and disgust for him.

She got up from the chair. "It's no use," she said. "As soon as the police come and I've told my story, I'm leaving."

He stood with her, those odd eyes burning again. He stared at her in grim silence a moment. "If you turn me down in this you are a fool! I could make you famous! The envy of Venice and the world!"

It was clear to her now that he was insane. His suave front could not hide that. Jeffrey had been right in his warnings. All she wanted was to escape. The remembrance of poor Arnold's broken body stretched out on the patio at the rear of the castle sickened her. She had lost a young man who had truly loved her and in a very real sense given his life for her. She would always be haunted by guilt for his death.

Her unhappy reverie was broken by the sound of an angry voice and a clamoring at the entrance door to the castle. She at once assumed it was the police and tried to collect herself to be able to tell her account of what had taken place. She saw the grim look on Quentin's face as he left her and marched out into the entrance hall to answer the door. A liveried servant appeared to take care of the task, but Quentin silently waved him off and went to the door himself.

When he opened it Anita was shocked to see that it was not the police but her brother, Jeffrey. Shock was followed by relief and she rushed forward to him with open arms, crying, "Jeffrey!"

He turned to her in anger. "So you are here! You lied to me! I found it out by questioning the gondolier when he returned to the hotel. He told me the restaurant he'd taken you to!" There was scathing bitterness in his words and on his face.

"Please don't go over all that!" she begged him, on the edge of hysteria now. "Something dreadful has happened."

"Indeed," Jeffrey said acidly. "I'm not at all surprised. And where is Arnold? He has some explaining to do for his part in the lie."

She swallowed hard. "Arnold is dead."

Jeffrey stared at her in startled silence for a moment. Then in a different tone, he said, "I can't have heard you right."

"Arnold is dead. He fell or was pushed down a steep flight of marble steps."

Her brother turned to Quentin for the first time. The young master of the castle had been standing by silently. Now Jeffrey asked him, "Is what my sister says true?"

Quentin hesitated, a nerve in his cheek twitching perceptibly. Then in a calm voice, he said, "I regret that Miss Burgess seems to be confused."

"Confused?" Jeffrey said irritably. "You haven't answered my question? Is anything wrong with Arnold Tenn?"

Quentin shrugged. "I couldn't say."

"Couldn't say?" Jeffrey repeated.

Anita turned to the suddenly cold and aloof Quentin. "Tell him the truth!" she demanded. "Tell him what happened! How Arnold and Mara went on a tour of the castle. Later we heard a scream. When we rushed out she was at the top of the rear marble stairway in a kind of trance and Arnold was stretched out at the foot of the stairs in a pool of blood!" Her voice broke as she finished.

Jeffrey listened with his face shadowing with anger. "What about all that, Quentin?"

"Some kind of mad imaginings on your sister's part," Quentin said with a brazenness that Anita found hard to believe.

She told her brother, "He's lying!"

Jeffrey frowned at her. "I realize one of you has to be," he said. And he addressed himself to Quentin again, "Where is Arnold now?"

"I've already told you. I don't know," Quentin said showing a sneering smile on his face.

"It's obvious he came here with my sister," Jeffrey told him. "What happened to him?"

"Part of the story Miss Burgess told you was right. Arnold left the castle in company of Mara. They went away together somewhere. Your sister was very upset at their going and developed this hysteria. Probably because of jealousy."

"Is this true?" Jeffrey asked her.

She was aghast at Quentin's unexpected behavior. And she was too confused to defend herself properly. Near tears, she cried, "No! All he's saying is a lie! Arnold is out there on the patio dead! Go see for yourself!"

Jeffrey was frowning. "I think I will," he said evenly. "What about it, Collins?"

Quentin shrugged. "It's ridiculous. There's no basis to what she says."

"Still I would like to go out there," Jeffrey insisted.

Quentin appeared reluctant and Anita felt that she had won the battle after all. She grasped her brother's arm as she glared angrily at the young master of the castle. "Make him take you out there! You'll see I'm telling the truth!"

"I insist on seeing the stairs and that patio," Jeffrey told Quentin.

"Very well," Quentin said in a quiet voice. "But you will merely make a fool of yourself."

"I'm willing to risk that," was Jeffrey's grim reply. And to her, he said, "I want you to come along."

Quentin marched ahead of them down the high corridors with their archways and ornate marble inlay. He held his shoulders straight and his stride was firm. Anita clung to her brother, her eyes moist with tears and her entire body afflicted with a small trembling.

They passed the entrance to the shadowed dining room where the candles still flickered on the white-clothed table and the remains of the elaborate dinner. Then they stepped out onto the patio overlooking the canal.

Quentin went as far as the bottom of the steep marble stairway and halted. Then he turned to them with a sneering expression. "Is this the spot?"

Jeffrey halted and looked at her with a questioning frown. "Well?"

She was speechless. Arnold's body had vanished and so had the blood.

"He was there!" She cried finally, pointing to the place where she had last seen her fiance.

"He's not there now," Jeffrey said in a suspicious voice that made her realize he was ready to accept Quentin's version of the affair rather than hers.

She gazed accusingly at Quentin Collins. "You had him moved while we were in the living room? You arranged it while we were talking. And I don't suppose you called the police at all?"

Quentin smiled at her coldly. "Why should I call the police? I can't dictate to Mara where she goes or who she goes out with. If you want to send the police looking for the two of them you can. I'll have no part in it."

Jeffrey gave Quentin a sharp look. "I hope you're telling the truth, Collins. If you're not you won't get away with this."

"It's murder!" Anita sobbed brokenly. "And he's covering it up!"

Quentin rolled his eyes in a gesture of annoyed resignation. "I have never had much patience with hysterical young women," he said. "I wish you'd get your sister out of here, Burgess."

It was the final humiliation and sent her across to him pounding her fists on his chest and crying out that he was a murderer. She was beyond any restraint or knowing what she was saying. She had endured too much and the very sight of him was more than she could stand.

She was vaguely aware of Jeffrey shouting in her ear. Then he had grasped her and was drawing her away from the slightly shocked Quentin. All the while she kept sobbing out accusations against him. Jeffrey tried to calm her with reasoning words, but she paid no attention to him. He was forced to physically propel her along the corridor to the entrance of the castle and out into the semi darkness of the landing. She was conscious of the curious expression on the face of the waiting gondolier as Jeffrey literally pushed her down into the craft. She lay in the darkness of the boat sobbing during the trip along the canal to their hotel.

In the suite of their hotel, fortified with a cup of strong tea she repeated her account of the tragedy to a scowling Jeffrey. She ended with, "I'm positive poor Arnold is dead. I knelt by his body. Touched his cold forehead."

"According to Collins, the girl and Arnold went off somewhere together."

"He made it all up."

"Then what can have happened to Arnold's body?" Jeffrey demanded.

"He's done something with it. Likely dumped it into the canal. Anything to divert suspicion from him."

Jeffrey gave her a reproving look. "It all comes from your being so stubborn. I warned you against Quentin Collins and that house with its strange cult."

"I know," she admitted tearfully.

"Now when we should be leaving Italy we are faced with this unhappy business," he grumbled. "And if Arnold should be dead it will be hard to explain to his family. And you have lost a fiance."

"You must talk to the authorities at once," she insisted. "He said he'd send a message to the police. But he didn't."

Jeffrey halted before her with a deep sigh. "The language problem makes it difficult to get through to the police. I had better call on the American Consulate for help, though I'll be in a pretty predicament if Arnold and that girl should turn up alive and well."

"You still think he may be telling you the truth?"

"I don't know what to think any longer," Jeffrey admitted worriedly.

She gave a tiny shudder as she stared at the crimson carpet of the suite's living room. She said, "The last time I saw Arnold alive he was walking out of the room with Mara. Whenever he was with her she seemed to exert some strange kind of spell over him. He left without even asking my permission. And that wasn't like him."

"And you were alone with Collins?"

"Yes. It was then I began to realize how right you had been about him."

"A little late."

"But he had seemed so pleasant before. Now he began to urge me to join his cult. He said he needed someone like me to complete his circle."

"His circle of witches," Jeffrey said bitterly. "All Venice knows that black magic is practiced in that house."

"There is something about his eyes. I think he has the power to hypnotize. That perhaps I'd been partially hypnotized by him from the time of my first meeting with him. But his cruelty broke the spell. I was frightened. And he upset me more by telling a gruesome story about Mara."

"About Mara?"

"Yes," she nodded. "He said she was suffering from the Gorgon curse. That at times her beauty changed to a face of such ugly horror that it could cause those who saw it to die of shock."

"Ridiculous! He was trying to intimidate you with scary stories."

"I don't know," she worried. "I think he was saying that she had an insane streak and sometimes it showed. That when she had one of those spells she might kill. And I think that is what happened tonight. In one of her mad frenzies she turned on Arnold and shoved him down the steps!"

Her brother showed disbelief. "I've heard so many tall tales about it I'm at a loss!"

"The sure facts are that he did somehow topple down the stairs to his death," she said. "And Mara and Quentin were somehow involved in it. The authorities should be asked to investigate."

Jeffrey looked unhappy. "I'll have to go and try to rouse the American consul," he said. "I know there is no way of trying to get to the bottom of this without his help."

"You mustn't lose any time for Arnold's sake," she pleaded.

He looked grim. "What does it matter if he's already murdered?"

"There's a slim chance he might be alive," she said. "I only examined him for a moment. They could have hidden him in the castle somewhere. He might be dying alone in the darkness there."

Her brother showed increasing concern. "You paint a desperate picture," he said. "I'll have to somehow find means to persuade the police to search that castle from top to bottom. And that may not be easy."

He left her with continued grumblings. But she knew he would do his best, and he was resourceful in things of this sort. She prayed that Arnold might be spared. Alone in the suite her long vigil began. She was too nervous to go to bed. For a while she paced about the room. Then she sat in a large easy chair and dozed for a time. But she was soon awake. When dawn came to light, the noble buildings casting a pinkish glow on their marble facades, she was standing forlornly at one of the windows.

It was several hours later before a thoroughly weary and bitter Jeffrey returned. He gave her a questioning look. "Haven't you slept at all?" he asked.

"Would you expect me to?"

"No," he sighed as he slumped in a chair. Then he gazed up at her, the dark circles under his eyes very apparent. "I finally managed to get some cooperation from the police," he said. "They're going to raid the palace and search it. I had to do some tall storytelling, indicating Quentin Collins had attacked you and taken Arnold prisoner. If they discover I've been lying it could land me in prison here."

"You haven't exaggerated all that much," she said. "Quentin Collins did handle me roughly and he has to be behind what happened to Arnold."

"The American consul is very angry," Jeffrey went on with a sigh. "He doesn't like to get mixed up in such things. He's known for some time that Collins has been carrying on some kind of fiendish practices in that castle with all those girls. And he's heard the rumors of how the ancient owner of it was probably murdered yet he's chosen to avoid accusing Quentin. Now he has no choice."

Anita stared at her brother. "What do you think will happen?"

"If I know Collins he'll lie his way out of it."

"I hope not," she said tensely. "He's an evil man. He shouldn't be at large."

"First we'll have to wait for word of the raid," Jeffrey told her. "Right now we should have some sort of breakfast."

Word came about the raid shortly after they finished breakfast. It was brought by no less a personage than Alexander Carr, Dorothy's father, and one of the prominent Americans of the Venice expatriate colony.

He was a lanky man with gray hair and black eyebrows the most prominent feature in a long, rather pale face with a pained expression. The pain was especially prominent on his features as he addressed himself to them.

"The authorities raided the castle," he informed him. "And they found no sign of Arnold Term or the girl, Mara. They questioned Quentin Collins and some of the girls belonging to his cult who share the castle with him. They all bear out his story that Mara left the castle in company with Arnold Tenn."

"He's put them up to that," she told Dorothy's father. Alexander Carr looked uncomfortable.

"Possibly," he said. "But the consul now seems to agree that Quentin Collins has been telling the truth. He believes your fiance and this Mara girl have gone off somewhere."

"Arnold wouldn't do that," she declared.

Alexander Carr spread his hands in embarrassment. "It is not unknown for young men to do peculiar things in strange surroundings. Venice is a lush city and I understand that girl, Mara, was strikingly beautiful. It could be one of those passing affairs."

Jeffrey gave the older man a stern look. "I agree with my sister. Arnold Tenn was too level-headed for anything of that nature. I'm sorry the police raid produced no results."

Carr sighed. "Under the circumstances perhaps the best

thing to do would be to leave Venice without creating any further stir. In due time it is likely young Tenn will show up and follow you on to the next city."

Jeffrey said, "We'll think about that. But I should imagine the police would have a case against Quentin Collins for his black magic activities. He is the focal point of gossip in the city. What goes on in that house is whispered about at every gathering."

The older man looked gloomy. "I dare say Collins will overstep himself one of these days. Until he does one can only wait."

And wait they did. Anita refused to leave Venice. And for once her brother didn't try to dissuade her from what she wanted to do. The heat continued. On one of those sweltering afternoons a huge box was delivered to her. It was from Quentin Collins! A box filled with cut roses! The odor of the delicate flowers brought back memories of the castle and made her feel ill. The card with the flowers simply bore the name of the suave young American.

She had a maid take the flowers away at once. She could tell that the girl was puzzled by her dislike of the bouquet. It was one of those things difficult to explain to others.

She was seated by the window when the door of the suite opened and Jeffrey came in. He had a kind of haggard air about him that at once made her think there had been some news.

She jumped up from her chair and went to meet him. Staring into his haunted eyes, she said, "You've heard something."

"Yes," he said in a taut voice.

"What?"

His young face was lined and grim. "Two bodies were found in the canal not far from Castle Asariana this morning."

"Two bodies?"

"Yes. One was Arnold's. And the other was that of Mara."

"Mara!" she gasped in astonishment.

He nodded. "Her throat had been cut from ear to ear!"

CHAPTER 4

A t this announcement Anita, filled with an aching sense of loss, sank down on a nearby divan. She had begun to hope that Arnold might not really be dead, that he would be found locked in some hidden room of the castle. But the discoveries of the two bodies eliminated any chance of this.

She glanced up at Jeffrey. "Surely the authorities will take some action against Quentin Collins now."

"I'm sure that they will," he said. "This brings the entire scandal of his black magic activities into the spotlight. They'd do well to step in before there are more murders."

Anita frowned. "I'm sure that Mara was under drugs or hypnosis. Perhaps both. Quentin made her do his bidding without argument. He holds the same sinister power over all those other beautiful girls of his black magic cult."

"And he wanted you to join the group and live at the castle," Jeffrey said.

"Yes," she said quietly. "To try to make me do that, he decided to kill Arnold. I accuse Quentin of killing him because he directed Mara to do it."

"Why was the girl murdered?" her brother asked.

"I suppose to keep her from talking," she said. "I have an idea she was really fond of Arnold and may have regretted what she did.

She went into a fit of hysterics when Quentin Collins brought her out of that spell. He quickly took her away. I wondered then."

"If they do raid the castle again and arrest Collins it is possible we may be forced to remain here to appear as witnesses against him," Jeffrey warned her.

"I think we should if there is any chance of bringing him to justice," Anita said.

"We'll have to wait and see what happens," her brother sighed.

What happened might have been expected, knowing Quentin Collins as they did. Word of it was revealed to them during a dinner party at Alexander Carr's Venetian mansion a few evenings later. The lanky millionaire summoned them to his library for a private discussion. His daughter, Dorothy, was also included in the secret conversation. When they were all four in the darkly elegant room and seated, the millionaire addressed them across his mahogany desk.

His long face was serious as he announced, "The raid on Quentin Collins' castle was carried out late this afternoon."

Jeffrey, seated on the arm of Dorothy's chair, showed excitement at the news. "What was the result?" he asked.

Alexander Carr looked grim. "Disappointing."

"In what way?" Anita asked from her chair near the desk.

The gray-haired man gave her a bleak glance. "When the police forced their way into the castle it was empty."

"Empty?" Jeffrey echoed.

"Quentin and all his group had vanished. They must have been told what was going to happen," Alexander Carr said bitterly. "There are often leaks in the police department here. I'm afraid some of its members are corrupt. In any event the castle was deserted."

Anita grimaced. "I'm not surprised. Quentin realized he might have to face murder charges. He had nothing to gain by remaining."

"The worst feature of it all is that it places a dark stain on the good name of the local American colony," Alexander Carr worried. "It will take some time for Collins and his dark actions to be forgotten."

His daughter, Dorothy, spoke up, "We can live it down. But the really awful thing is that he caused a fellow countryman to be murdered and he seemingly will not suffer for his crime."

"Quentin Collins is undoubtedly on his way out of Italy at this moment," her father said. "The chances of the law catching up with him are small."

Jeffrey's thin, intelligent face was grim. "It is time we started back to Philadelphia," he said. "We'll cancel out the balance of our tour and find a ship sailing directly to the United States."

The older man behind the desk nodded sympathetically. "I know how you and your sister must feel."

"We'll take Arnold's body with us," Jeffrey said. "And we'll try to explain the circumstances of his death to his family. The facts are so fantastic it won't be easy."

"I have an idea several journalists will be writing news stories about Quentin, his coterie of lovely girls in that black magic circle and the murders," Alexander Carr said. "It is too sensational not to attract an international readership."

Anita sighed. "I am most to blame. I forced him to go to the castle with me."

Dorothy rose from her chair and went over to her, placing an understanding hand on her shoulder, and saying, "That isn't completely true. Arnold was fascinated by Mara. I doubt if he would have been so willing to go if he hadn't looked forward to seeing her again."

Alexander Carr from his desk agreed. "That unfortunate young man was in the girl's company a good deal the night of the ball."

Dorothy sighed. "If the truth be told we all share guilt. How many of us refused to attend that ball? Yet we all knew Quentin Collins was engaged in evil in that house."

Jeffrey stood up. "I doubt that post-mortems will ever place the blame fairly. I surely don't think Anita should take it all on her shoulders. We can only hope that one day the law will catch up with Quentin Collins."

"I agree," Alexander Carr said solemnly. "Though I would say he will have to be caught in some other crime. The chances of proving him guilty here are small."

During the next several days Jeffrey Burgess was kept busy making arrangements to leave the city of canals. The scandal centered around Quentin Collins and the murders was raging, and the American colony in Venice was in a furor. There were all sorts of wild rumors as to what had happened to the evil young man from Maine and his selected group of young women dedicated to the worship of Satan. Some claimed they had left in a ship bound for Morocco and planned to establish a new headquarters there.

Anita wanted only to escape from the reminders of those last happy days with Arnold and the gossip that was raging about the murders. The charm of the ancient city held no more magic for her. She found the continued heat that had plagued the ancient city so strangely for many weeks more enervating than ever. Much of the time she spent in the hotel.

Jeffrey returned one day with the good news they would be

leaving the following morning. "I have found a vessel going directly to New York from Genoa," he told her. "We will take the train to Genoa in the morning."

"What about Arnold's body?" she asked.

He frowned. "It will make the journey along with us on both the train and ship. I have had it placed in a leaded coffin so there will be no problems."

Anita at once sent a message to her friend, Dorothy Carr, advising of their planned departure. Later, in response, Dorothy had a messenger return with a note requesting that Anita meet her at St. Mark's Square on the Grand Canal at two o'clock.

She left the hotel a few minutes before the appointed time and was waiting in that crowded place which is the heart and soul of Venice just as the two Moors, on the Palace of the Doges, struck the hour on the giant chimes of its clock. She strained to see Dorothy's familiar face among the crowd, expecting to be joined by her and taken for refreshment to one of the many small restaurants that bordered the alleyways near the palace.

Tourists and natives were standing near the flagpoles from which were flying the banner of St. Mark and the tricolor of Italy. Everyone used the square as a sort of outdoor living room. They met and talked and fed the pigeons which were always part of the scene.

She hadn't recovered from the grim experiences of the past weeks, and as she stood there in the warm sunlight amid the chattering crowds, she began to feel nervous and weak. She wished that her girlfriend would come. Being there alone made her uneasy. All at once there was a tugging at her skirt and she looked down into the smiling, olive-skinned face of a barefooted youngster.

"Signorina Burgess?" the boy inquired.

She nodded. "Si!"

The boy indicated the area of the alley ways with a jerk of his head and still smiling tugged at her skirt for her to follow him. She at once decided that Dorothy was waiting for her somewhere over there and had sent the boy to fetch her. Dorothy spoke Italian fairly well.

"I'll come along with you," she told the boy, making a gesture so that he would understand.

He nodded happily and led the way for her, glancing back every few seconds and smiling up at her, to be sure that he had not lost her. They brushed through the knots of people crowding the square and finally reached one of the dark little alleys. The boy smiled at her again and led her a short distance to the entrance of a shop whose windows were filled with examples of fine glassware. The boy pointed inside.

Anita thanked him and gave him a coin. Then she entered

the shadowed musty smelling little shop. There was no proprietor in sight as she advanced to one of the counters to examine the goods. She wondered if he might have taken Dorothy to another room to a different display of the shop's offerings.

A floorboard creaked behind her and a hand seized her arm. She turned with fear in her eyes to look up into the grim face of Quentin Collins. She gasped.

"You!" she said.

He offered her a faint, mocking smile. "Didn't you expect to see me again?"

"Only if the police had caught up with you," she said as his grip pinched her arm painfully.

"Yes. That was awkward," he said.

"They said you had left Venice!"

"I'll be doing that shortly," he assured her. "But I wanted to see you before I left. Happily I noticed you on the square just now."

"Let me go!" she begged him.

"In good time," he said. "I have you and your brother to thank for spoiling things for me here."

"You have the murders and other evil you've committed to blame for that," she told him.

"You must get that out of your head," he frowned. "I did not murder Arnold Tenn. It was an accident."

"What about Mara?"

"She was a suicide. You were there that night. You know how the accident upset her. She blamed herself for the death of your fiance."

Anita regarded him bitterly. "A likely story! And how did their bodies get so conveniently in the canal?"

"I was responsible for that," he admitted. "I knew the police were waiting for a chance to crack down on my operation at the castle. I didn't want to have them poking around there investigating an accident and a suicide. I was afraid they would try to prove them murders and point an accusing finger at me."

"Rightly so," she told him.

He eyed her with annoyance. "You don't give up an idea easily, do you?"

"Not in this case."

"You were wrong not to join me," he told her. And then his eyes moved to the door of the small shop and a look of alarm crossed his pleasant face. Without another word he released his hold on her arm and swiftly went to the back of the shop where he vanished behind a hanging curtain of drab brown in a narrow doorway.

Startled and relieved she turned to see Dorothy entering the front door of the glassware shop. The redhead showed a look of amazement on her pretty face. "Why did you come here?" she asked. Anita advanced to her. "How did you know?"

"I was just getting out of a gondola when I saw you following the little boy in this direction. I didn't understand and decided I had better come after you."

She turned to glance at the still swaying brown curtain in the rear doorway where Quentin had disappeared. Then, trembling, she told Dorothy. "It was Quentin Collins. He saw me and sent the boy to bring me here. I thought the lad was a messenger of yours so I came with him."

Dorothy glanced at the rear of the shop with apprehension. "Quentin!"

As she finished speaking the brown curtain was pushed aside and an old hunchbacked man joined them, smiling. "There is something the Signorinas would like to see?"

Anita stared at the little man with his beard-stubbled, sly face. "Where is he?" she demanded. "Quentin Collins?"

The hunchback stared up at her. "Quentin Collins," he repeated in a puzzled tone. "I have not heard the name before."

"The man who was here before you came," Dorothy told him sharply.

The little man spread his hands and smiled stupidly. "There is no one but me here," he assured her.

"We'll get nowhere with him," Dorothy warned her. "Let us go!"

She required no urging. Hastily they left the dark and musty little shop and fairly raced down the shadowed cobblestoned alley towards the square. Once Anita glanced back to see if they were being followed but there was no sign of anyone.

Breathless when they reached the square and its crowds, she asked her friend, "Shouldn't we try to get the police and have them go back there in search of Quentin?"

Dorothy shook her head. "Useless. He's gone by now. And that old man in the shop is undoubtedly in his pay."

"It means Quentin Collins is still in the city," she pointed out. "The police should be told that."

"I'd keep out of it," Dorothy warned her. "It could end with your being asked to remain here and that would ruin all the plans Jeffrey has made for getting away in the morning."

"I suppose so," she said doubtfully.

"Be wise," her friend told her. "You were fortunate enough to escape him again. Let it go at that. Come, we'll find the restaurant I'd planned to take you to. Then we can talk it over quietly."

The restaurant was in another of the many alleys. It was a quiet, pleasant place and they were the only customers at this early afternoon period. Over pastries and coffee Anita told her friend everything that Quentin had said. How he had continued to insist he had no part in the murders.

"It's an outside chance," Dorothy said. "But I wouldn't place much faith in anything he told you. Of course he was in trouble because of his black magic practices. And he knew any other complications would ruin the work of his cult."

"That's true," Anita sighed.

"My suggestion is that you go back to the United States and try to forget what happened here. You'll probably never learn the truth and dwelling on it will only make you unhappy."

"I'll never be able to forget Arnold and that he lost his life here," Anita grieved.

"That is going to take time," her friend said sympathetically. "But be sure he would not want you to give your life up to mourning. You must start to build again."

"I'll try," Anita said.

"And forget about Quentin Collins. Even if he wasn't guilty of any crimes in the case of the deaths of Arnold and Mara, he contributed to the atmosphere that caused them. He is an evil man and he'll always be the cause of misfortune for some."

Anita thought her friend had summed it up very well. Later they parted after saying their goodbyes and she went straight back to the hotel. She had made up her mind to tell Jeffrey of her brief meeting with Quentin and warn him of the complications they might face if she reported the incident to the police.

Jeffrey listened to her story when he returned to the suite. His thin face was dark with anger. "The nerve of that devil!" he cried. "If Dorothy hadn't come he might have kidnapped you."

"I doubt it," she said. "But I think he did want to have his say. Tell his side of the murders."

"Of course he was lying again," Jeffrey said angrily. "If we hadn't all our tickets bought and passage booked on that ship I would take the risk of telling the police."

"It probably isn't worth it. He's safely on his way wherever he's going by now."

"I suppose so," Jeffrey said. "We can't be delayed. So we're bound to silence."

They said goodbye to Venice the following morning. As she waited by the train Anita had a glimpse of Arnold's specially sealed coffin on a cart being wheeled to the baggage car. She turned away from it with tears brimming in her eyes once more. Jeffrey came to join her and help her aboard the train. The journey to Genoa was long and tiring. From there they transferred briefly to a hotel. The following day they went to the ship that was taking them back to

America. They did not do any exploring of the proud city where Christopher Columbus was born.

The journey across the Atlantic was uneventful and most noteworthy for its good weather. In a blue mood Anita kept to herself, making few friends among the other passengers. Jeffrey was also subdued and thoughtful. As they came near the end of the voyage she thought more of the young man whose body rested somewhere down in the hold of the ship in the special coffin. There would be great unhappiness for his parents and relatives, and she would be experiencing the tragedy of his death all over again.

On the day before landing she and Jeffrey talked about this. Her brother said, "Arnold was my close friend as well as your fiance. I do not intend to allow his death to go unavenged."

She stared at him as they stood at an isolated section of the ship's rail. "What have you in mind?"

"I don't just know. But I will develop some plan," he said.

"I doubt if we shall ever see Quentin Collins again."

Her brother's face was grim. "Don't be too sure of that. And lately I've been wondering about Mara."

"What about her?"

"If she was such a close colleague of Quentin's I'm surprised that he was so careless as to allow her to suicide. I wonder if he didn't find some unfortunate look-alike and have her murdered and her body placed in the canal to make it seem the girl was a suicide. They identified the body chiefly by clothing and jewelry."

Anita was startled by this suggestion. "I'd never given such a possibility a thought."

"It's been bothering me," Jeffrey said. "I can't help thinking the girl may still be alive."

"I suppose anything is possible. The people in that castle were so weird. And Quentin told me that horrifying story about her having spells and her appearance changing to shocking ugliness."

"I remember. He spoke of the Gorgon curse. You felt he was being symbolic. That he meant she was tainted with madness and during her insane spells was capable of violent criminal acts."

She smiled bitterly. "I can't picture any face, however dreadful, striking men dead."

"It goes back to mythology, the Medusa legend," her brother said. "The Gorgon is always a beautiful woman who at times is subject to macabre facial distortion."

"I had never heard of the legend before," she said.

"I suppose it doesn't matter," her brother sighed. "Mara is presumably dead. Whatever strange affliction she suffered from has no importance any longer."

So the discussion of Mara and her fate was dropped. But later

Anita was to think about it and wonder. Long months would pass before this came about and in the interval her sorrow for Arnold would have lost its edge.

Fall and winter came and passed. Anita knew that her brother had kept up a correspondence with Alexander Carr in Italy. He'd mentioned to her that there had been no further word of Quentin in Venice. She'd not been surprised though the memory of his good-looking face and sinister magnetism still stayed with her.

And then as the pleasant, warm afternoons of spring arrived Jeffrey came to her private sitting room one day in a high state of excitement. She had been sitting by a window overlooking the garden, sewing. She at once gave her attention to Jeffrey as he paced up and down before her.

"I have found out where Quentin Collins is," he announced.

"Oh?"

He stared at her in astonishment. "You don't seem to care? I was sure you'd be as interested as I am."

She sighed and stared at the sewing in her lap. "I've been trying to forget last summer and what it meant to me."

"I can never forget," her brother said angrily. "You may be willing to call accounts closed in the loss of your fiance but I'm not ready to so lightly dismiss the murder of a friend."

Hurt came to her eyes. "Please," she said. "You know I loved Arnold. These long months since his death have only made that more apparent."

"Then my news should be important to you," Jeffrey said with a frown.

"Go on," she said, "I'm listening."

"He is living in Collinsport in Maine."

"That is his home village, isn't it?"

"The seat of the Collins family," her brother went on. "And Quentin has returned to live at the family estate of Collinwood on the death of his older brother. He is acting the role of respectable country gentleman."

"Perhaps he has reformed," she suggested. "Some wild young men do. He may have learned his lesson."

"I strongly doubt that," Jeffrey said. "And now that I have located him I'm going ahead with my plan to make him pay for Arnold Tenn's death."

She studied him worriedly. "I no longer am sure that vengeance is desirable," she said. "I'm afraid of what it may do to you. To us."

"Too late to have doubts. I've settled all the arrangements. I have rented a guest cottage on the estate of Collinwood and you and I are going to spend the summer there."

She sat forward in her chair. "I couldn't!" she gasped. "I don't want to ever see Quentin Collins again."

"You will. It is part of my plan."

"What plan?"

Jeffrey smiled coldly. "I'm going to use his methods. I'm going to pretend I've forgiven him for Venice. That I'm anxious to be friendly with him. I used an assumed name when I rented the cottage from his lawyer. So our coming will be a complete surprise."

"Quentin will never believe in your wishes for friendship with him," she warned Jeffrey.

"I think he will."

"Why?"

"Because it will be what he wants to believe," her brother said. "And people are quick to convince themselves of what appeals to them."

She was troubled by his manner and all that he was saying. He had become obsessed with this unpleasant idea. "Quentin is evil and much cleverer than you," she worried. "You'll not deceive him."

"The fact you are with me will help. He won't be looking for me to expose you to his villainy. I'm counting on you to make friends with him as well and help me trap him."

"I don't think I can go through with it," she protested.

"You must," Jeffrey snapped. "Otherwise Quentin Collins may pass the rest of his days living the life of a peaceful country gentleman. He needs to be searched out and made to pay for his evil."

"There was talk in Venice that he had the power to transform his body to that of a werewolf. Do you feel strong enough to combat all the powers of black magic he may possess?"

"I'm not afraid of him if that's what you mean."

"I admire your courage," she said. "But he may still be conducting a group dedicated to Satan. You may discover you have more than one adversary."

"From all I've heard he returned to Collinwood alone. None of his group are with him."

She stared at him. "I can see that you're going through with this no matter what I say."

He nodded. "Yes. Even if you refuse to accompany me."

"I won't do that. I'm too frightened you may come to harm," she said. "At least I can share the danger with you."

Jeffrey brightened. "There need be no danger if we play our cards properly. I'll pretend friendship until I get the information I want. And then Quentin Collins may have exactly the kind of accident that lost us Arnold."

Her eyebrows lifted. "You're planning to kill him?"

"I'd rather you phrased it as arranged an accident," Jeffrey said. "For that is what it must seem."

"Need you resort to becoming a murderer in the name of justice?"

"At the moment I can think of no other way," her brother said with a shrug. "Though it is possible I may get enough evidence of his criminal past to force him to suicide or disgrace. I would prefer such alternatives."

"And so would I," she said.

"But we will have to let that work out when we get there. Meanwhile, you'll be charming to him."

She gave a tiny shudder. "That won't be easy."

"You can force yourself."

"When do you expect to leave Philadelphia for Maine?"

"In a week or two," he said. "I'll admit I'm impatient. I want to go as soon as possible."

"Very well," she said wearily. "I'll arrange my plans so that I can accompany you."

"I dislike making you take the risk," he admitted. "But I feel it is necessary to the success of the project."

"I don't mind," she said.

"Quentin isn't entirely surrounded by friends," her brother went on. "I hear his cousin, Barnabas Collins, is also visiting the estate. He is staying at what is called the old house. And the rumor goes that while he and Quentin maintain an outward politeness when they meet, they actually hate each other."

CHAPTER 5

They reached Collinsport on a dark, fog-ridden midnight on the coastal boat that made the journey from Boston. Standing with her brother on the deck of the boat as it approached the wharf of the Maine village, Anita feared the unpleasant weather might be an ominous warning of what lay ahead of them there.

Lanterns were set out on the wharf to give light for the unloading and loading of the coastal steamer. She could see hogsheads lined up to be rolled onto the boat and there were wagons waiting and a scattered group of men and women standing there in the foggy darkness.

On the trip from Boston she and Jeffrey had become friendly with a young man from Collinsport, David Benson, who had gone to Boston where he studied law. He was now returning to the village for an extended holiday. He was a warm, intelligent young man with a broad, friendly face. Hearing that they were to get off at Collinsport and spend the summer at Collinwood he became talkative.

They sat together at a table in the dining salon. And in the lamp-lit atmosphere of the crowded room with its bevy of waiters and odor of good food, he filled them in on the history of the village.

"My family have only been there for a few years," he told them. "But the Collins family founded the village. And they've pretty well run it ever since. They own the main industry, the fish-packing plant, the general store and the hotel. I hear they also have a share in the Blue Whale Tavern, though they won't admit to that."

Anita had smiled faintly. "They prefer complete respectability."

"They do," the young lawyer agreed. "And now I understand that Quentin Collins has returned to head the family."

"We heard the same thing," Jeffrey said, giving Anita a knowing glance as he tried to get information from the stranger. "Just what sort of person is he?"

"I don't know him too well," the young man said. "I met him a few times about four years ago when he was home on a visit. He struck me as being rather secretive."

"That's interesting," Jeffrey said.

The young man frowned. "He had the reputation of being wild. But that's only too easy to come by in a village such as Collinsport. I heard some odd rumors about him. But now he seems to have returned in honor."

"Is Collinwood far from the village?" she asked.

"A few miles out," the young man said. "But it has a fine location overlooking the ocean. And the cottage you've rented is only a stone's throw from the main house."

"What about the old house?" Jeffrey asked.

The young man smiled. "That was the original Collinwood. It's further back from the sea, close to the family cemetery. It is a smaller building than the new Collinwood. But though I've never been in it I believe it is still in good repair."

"It must be," Jeffrey said dryly. "I understand that a cousin of the Collins family lives there at intervals."

"You mean Barnabas Collins," the young man said.

"Yes, I think that's his name," Anita smiled.

"Barnabas is more of a mystery to me than Quentin," the young man said frankly. "The few times I've met him were after dark. We'd meet on some country road or other. To be friendly I always spoke, but he never struck up a conversation. He's a very aloof man."

"We heard he was a much nicer person than Quentin," Anita's brother said.

Dave Benson considered this. "It could be that he is," he admitted. "He is an imposing-looking person. But I've been home so little in the last few years I've sort of gotten out of touch with things in the village."

"We're looking forward to our stay in Maine," Anita's brother told the young lawyer pleasantly.

"I hope so," David Benson had said with a smile. "And I'd like to show you and your sister some of the fine country around the village."

"That would be very nice," she said agreeably. Thus far she liked what she knew of the young man.

Now as the boat drew close to the wharf David Benson came out on deck to join her and Jeffrey. The young man smiled and said, "I'm afraid this isn't an ideal night for you to arrive. We can get spells of heavy fog here."

"It doesn't matter," she told the young man. "We're just wondering if a carriage has been sent to meet us. The lawyer promised there would be. But with it such a late hour you worry that they might have forgotten."

"If there isn't one from Collinwood I'll find one for you," David promised. "There are usually two or three rigs for hire waiting at the wharf."

Jeffrey turned to the young man. "You're very kind. And don't hesitate to call at our cottage at any time."

"I won't," he said.

The boat docked and they were among the six or seven passengers getting off at Collinsport. As they made their way up the rough wooden planks of the wharf, which were wet and slippery on this night of a foggy drizzle, a tall man with a mournful black moustache came forward and tipped his bowler hat to them.

"Would you be the new tenants of the Collinwood cottage?" he asked.

"Yes," Jeffrey said at once. "Have you been sent to meet us?"

"Yes, sir," the tall sad-looking man said. "And where would your luggage be?"

Jeffrey turned. "I believe they're just getting it off the boat now."

"I'll go see about it," the tall man in black said and tipped his hat as he continued on down the dock.

They moved forward towards the waiting carriages not sure which one would be theirs. As they did so they caught a glimpse of a regal-looking man wearing a caped coat, watching the activity on the wharf from a vantage point in the shadows. He had a handsome yet serious face. When he realized they had seen him he turned quickly and vanished into the night.

At the same moment David Benson joined them and indicated where the man had been standing with a nod, he said, "That was Barnabas Collins watching from up above the docks just now."

"We noticed him," Anita said. "He's very distinguished and handsome, but he must be terribly shy."

"He's often like that," David said. "But at least you'll know him if you see him again."

Jeffrey nodded. "He's not a type one would be liable to

forget."

"Very unusual fellow," David Benson agreed. "I see that Quentin Collins has sent Dolan to meet you. He's the estate coachman."

"Yes," Jeffrey said. "I have no idea which is our carriage. He didn't make that clear."

"The one with the brown horse. It has a mark like a white star on its nose," David said. "I at least remember that much. I'll say goodnight and I will see you again soon."

They expressed their pleasure in that and when he left them they moved on to the carriage he'd indicated. It was the right one, for shortly after, Dolan returned with his arms loaded with bags and a worker following behind him carrying the balance. With much puffing and effort the men loaded the bags onto the back of the carriage with several having to be placed inside where they would ride.

Dolan turned to them, still breathing heavily from his efforts. "We can leave any time now, sir," he said.

"Fine," Jeffrey said. "We're ready." And he helped her into the closed carriage. As they moved away from the docks they mounted a steep street paved with cobblestones and lined with nondescript one-story wooden buildings on either side of it.

Anita peered out through the somewhat grimy window of the carriage and learned that a building on the left was the general store. On the other side of the street, lights glowed from a tavern with a sign outside it announcing it as the Blue Whale. As the carriage creaked on up the sharp rise the buildings became more scattered.

Suddenly Anita touched her brother's arm for attention. "Look!" she said. She indicated the man in the caped coat walking along the left side of the road. He paid no attention to the carriage, moving slowly with his head slightly bent as if in deep thought.

"Barnabas Collins again," Jeffrey said as they passed him. "He does seem a solitary sort."

"He has a fine, strong face," Anita said.

Her brother nodded. "Young Benson seemed to approve of him." They were on a dark road now and the carriage began to jolt a good deal over its rough surface. He glanced at her in the shadowed interior and asked, "Well, what is your first impression of Collinsport?"

Her mood was bleak. "I think we have come a long way to receive small satisfaction. And perhaps land ourselves in both trouble and danger."

"You seem to have no confidence in me," he protested.

"I have no confidence in your purpose in coming here," she corrected him.

"Later you'll be congratulating me," he predicted.

She stared out the window at the bushes lining the road and made no reply. She had a feeling of some unknown menace that was threatening them. And she was afraid of the meeting they would have to have with Quentin.

After what seemed a long drive they halted before a pleasant stone cottage with a shingled roof. The driver got down from his perch and opened the door for them to get out. "This is the cottage, sir," he told Jeffrey.

Jeffrey stepped out into the damp gray night first and then helped her down to the gravel walk. She could see a large house with lights showing at many of its windows about fifty yards away. She asked the driver, "Is that Collinwood?"

"Yes, miss," Dolan said respectfully as he led the way to the cottage door with his arms loaded with bags. "That is the new house."

She was going to ask him about the other one but now he had opened the door and gone ahead with their luggage. She and Jeffrey followed him into a pleasant living room with a fireplace. There were a few partly burned logs in the fireplace and an enamel lamp in the center of a round table which in turn was in the middle of the plainly furnished room.

Dolan came back through a doorway at the side of the room. "Bedrooms and kitchen through this door," he said.

"Thank you," Jeffrey said. "I asked Mr. Collins' lawyer to see that the kitchen was stocked with some groceries."

"Been taken care of, sir," the driver said. "And one of the maids will come by with a can of fresh milk for you in the morning."

"It seems nothing has been overlooked," Jeffrey said. The driver had gone out to get the rest of their luggage. Anita went out through the door and found two bedrooms and a kitchen off a short hallway. The bedrooms were small and the kitchen only a fair size. But it would do. She hoped that Jeffrey would change his mind about revenge, and they would leave soon.

After Dolan had brought in the other bags, they were left alone. She was exhausted and bade Jeffrey a quick goodnight before going into the bedroom assigned to her. She began preparing for bed. She had just slipped into her nightgown when she realized she hadn't pulled the blind at the room's single window. She went rigid with a monstrous feeling of unseen eyes being fastened on her. Malevolent eyes working some kind of evil on her! She glanced in the direction of the window and sure enough she could just distinguish the shape of what seemed a cowled head and shoulders against the pattern of small panes!

Someone was out there spying on her! Someone in a weird

kind of black cowl! Fighting back her terror she forced herself to pretend to be starting across the room and then she quickly changed direction and rushed close to the window. The head and shoulders at once vanished but not so quickly that she couldn't follow the veiled figure as it moved off into the haze of fog and was lost.

With fear written on her pretty face she pulled down the blind. Who had it been? She couldn't even be sure whether it had been a man or a woman. But someone had been out there watching her and with a hatred so strong she had been able to sense it. Upset by this first unhappy experience she extinguished the candle on her dresser top and got into bed.

The macabre incident along with the ordeal of the night boat trip made her a prey to dreams when she finally fell asleep. Quentin Collins played a prominent part in most of them, always threatening her in some fashion. And in one particularly vivid nightmare Mara appeared with a taunting smile on her comely face. She had come close to her and then in a flash the dark girl's beauty had begun to transform into a mutilated grotesque face and her hair became tiny wriggling serpents. Anita raised her hands to stave off this gruesome horror and moaned in her sleep.

In the morning she wakened early to hear Jeffrey at the main door of the cottage engaged in a brisk conversation with someone. She listened and heard enough of what was being said to know it was the girl with the milk can.

She dressed quickly and joined her brother in the kitchen. It was a fine bright day and he was already engaged in preparing their breakfast. She at once took over the chores from him. While she worked she grasped the opportunity of telling him about her scare.

"A weird head and shoulders appeared at my bedroom window," she told him from the stove. "Someone was watching me as I prepared for bed."

"Are you sure?"

"Yes. I ran to the window in time to see them turn and rush off into the fog."

"It could have been shadows and your imagination," he warned her. "I know you were very tired when we arrived."

"I saw a head and shoulders seeming to be covered by a black cowl," she said with her brow wrinkled. "I'm sure it means bad luck. That we were wrong in ever coming here."

"I disagree," her brother said. "And I'd say your upset state gave you a kind of waking nightmare."

She saw there was no point in arguing with him. So she went about serving breakfast without mentioning the incident again. Jeffrey seemed very satisfied with the cottage. He'd already been outside for a stroll.

"Wonderful location," he said. "Close to the cliffs. And what a view of the bay and the ocean beyond. The Collins family made no mistake in selecting this site for their estate."

"It is rather isolated," she pointed out.

"Just far enough from the village for privacy," was his answer. "There's a path along the cliffs. But you must be careful. It goes close to the edge in places. And there's a frightening sheer drop from the edge to a rocky beach."

"I'll remember that."

"There's one place near the main house where the slope of the cliffs is much more gradual. There's a path that goes down to the beach, and a wharf with a few rowboats tied alongside it."

"The big house is very close," she said.

"Yes. The girl who came with the milk said it's only a three-minute walk. And it doesn't look to be any more."

She studied him across the breakfast table with solemn eyes. "I still say this is a mistake."

"You're wrong," he told her. Then he drank the last of his coffee. "We'll see who makes the first move."

"It's all very stupid!"

"Not if you remember Venice," her brother said, a hard expression coming to his intelligent face. "Quentin Collins has to be punished!"

They argued on a few minutes longer with neither of them coming closer to the other's point of view. Later as she was removing the dishes from the table to the sink there was a knock on the front door. They exchanged taut glances. Then Jeffrey rose slowly to answer the door.

She followed him into the living room and stood a distance back while he went over and drew the door open. And of course it was Quentin Collins, resplendent in gray country tweed, who stood out there. Seeing Jeffrey, a look of consternation crossed his face and he stepped inside.

"Jeffrey Burgess!" he said in amazement. "Did you rent the cottage?"

"Yes."

"You didn't give your own name," Quentin said accusingly.

"No," Jeffrey said, his chin raised in defiance. "I had an idea you mightn't welcome me if I did."

"But you chose to come anyway."

"Yes. I wanted to patch up my quarrel with you. And my sister feels the same way."

For the first time since his shock Quentin realized she also was there. He turned to her and then walked over and took her hand in his. He held it for a long moment, those hypnotic eyes meeting hers. "This makes it a truly delightful surprise," he said.

"I didn't think we should come," she said quietly.

The magnetic Quentin let go her hand and swung around to Jeffrey. "Of course it was a magnificent idea, your coming here. But how did you know I had returned to Collinwood?"

"I discovered it by chance," Jeffrey said casually. "And I felt I wanted to see you again. Partly to confess that I have decided we weren't fair to you in Venice. And to try and bring about some small friendship between us."

"That's extremely interesting," Quentin said. "But you really didn't have to make this generous gesture. I was wrong to a degree in Venice. I'm sure you'll agree with that, Anita."

She was embarrassed by this confrontation. She said, "All I have wanted to do is forget Venice and what happened there."

He nodded. "It was too bad about poor Arnold Tenn. And then I lost Mara as a result of his tragic accident. A bad business. And you were in error to cast the blame on me."

Jeffrey pretended to be troubled. "I have come to realize that only too well."

Quentin, who seemed to be enjoying the reminiscences and confession, moved across the room to Jeffrey again. "Yet I was leading a wicked existence in Italy. I had turned to Satan. My group of Devil worshipers were devout in their beliefs and loyal to me. And I revelled in my hold over those many lovely girls. I was drunk with my ability to sway them and anxious to use them to gain more power."

"I know nothing of that," Jeffrey protested.

"My vanity had betrayed me to the point of madness," the young master of Collinwood confessed to them with a worried expression on his youthful side-whiskered face. "You must have heard the gossip about my activities."

"You discount much of such talk."

"A lot of it was true," Quentin said with bitter frankness. "I did encourage my group to consider themselves a coven of witches and I did beg them to pay homage to Satan, Prince of Darkness."

"There is no need to confess so much," Jeffrey said. And she could tell that her brother was enjoying every minute of this and having a hard time concealing his triumph. His scheme was working much better than he'd hoped.

Quentin brushed aside Jeffrey's protest. "I want to be honest with you." And then he looked Anita's way. "And especially with you, my dear." She accepted his words with a feeling of revulsion, for she saw that most of this was pretense. That he also was playing some kind of macabre game. Both he and Jeffrey were indulging in grim charades.

She said, "I still say Venice is best forgotten."

"I am beginning to forget," Quentin assured her. "When the climax came I was actually thankful the police made it necessary for me to vanish. I had played the dangerous game too long. It was time for me to retire. There was no romance in my life with Mara lost to me. So I dismissed the members of my cult and came back here. My brother had died and it was my turn to assume responsibility for the family's affairs."

"And I'm positive you don't regret your reformation," Jeffrey said in his most friendly way.

"It was long overdue," Quentin said with mock sadness. "Now I must try to make up to you both for what I have done."

"You needn't," she said. "It is enough that you have decided on a new way of life."

"Trust my word on that," the young man said gravely. "Here in Collinsport I have the family's good name to uphold."

She asked, "Does anyone in the village know of your past?"

"No. I have been able to keep it a secret. And I trust neither of you will betray my sad history in Europe."

"We wouldn't dream of any such thing," Jeffrey said too quickly.

Quentin smiled his gratitude. "When I first saw you I was sure you had come here vindictively. Now I see that I was wrong."

"I think I have explained the feelings of my sister and myself."

"You have," Quentin agreed.

"We hope to enjoy our holiday here."

"I shall do all in my power to make it pleasant for you," Quentin assured them both.

"Are you living at the large house alone?" Jeffrey asked.

"No," Quentin said. "I have an uncle and a cousin with me. Also a lady friend of mine, recently widowed; her husband was close to me in my several years in Boston; and a young woman friend of my cousin. The house is large, some forty rooms in all. Both of you could have visited me as my guests if you'd let me know. Instead you rented this cottage in a false name!"

"We wish to be independent," Jeffrey said. "Because of the difficulties we experienced it is better for us not to rush things at first."

"Very well considered," Quentin said. And to Anita he added, "You must meet the rest of my family and friends. You and your brother will come to dinner with us at Collinwood tonight."

The prospect appalled her. "We have no wish to intrude," she said hastily.

"But I want you as my guests," he said grandly.

Jeffrey spoke up. "My sister and I will gladly accept your kind invitation. We must begin to show evidence of our sincerity. This would give us a fine chance to do so."

"Then it is settled," Quentin said with a glance her way for confirmation.

She gave a small resigned gesture to indicate it was all right. But she was too filled with unhappiness to speak.

She was thinking of that last dinner she'd had as his guest at the castle in Venice, and how disastrous that had turned out.

Jeffrey said, "On the night boat we met a David Benson who claimed to know you slightly."

Quentin nodded. "Yes. We've met. Isn't he a lawyer?"

"That's right," Jeffrey said.

"In Boston, I believe."

"He's come home for a holiday," Jeffrey explained. "I believe he had some illness during the winter, though he looks the picture of health now."

"Appearances can be deceiving," Quentin said lightly. Then he came over to her again. "As soon as you have settled in here you must let me show you the estate."

"Thank you," she said in a small voice.

Those hypnotic eyes studied her. "I have the feeling you may not have forgiven me," he said.

"I can't imagine why!" she protested.

"It's merely an impression," he said, still staring at her. "I'm sure I'm wrong."

"You are," she said, looking down to avoid his eyes.

"I have to be," Quentin said in his mocking fashion. "Otherwise what reason could you and your brother have for coming here to settle your differences with me?"

The irony in his voice convinced her that her brother had not deceived the evil Quentin Collins. It also made her feel certain that the young man's basic nature had not changed. She began to fear that rather than working out a crafty plan to turn the tables on Quentin, her overly confident brother had delivered them into a trap, a trap from which they could not easily escape with their lives.

There was an awkward moment of silence following Quentin's jeering question. The tension in the small living room of the cottage was grim, so grim that she felt she could scream out her fear.

Then Jeffrey said in his pseudo-friendly manner which she had already come to hate and distrust, "You need have no worry about our motives. And we'll anticipate the dinner and meet the others with a great deal of pleasure."

"Fine," Quentin said. "This has been a most interesting

encounter. Unexpected in every way for me. I'm sorry I must hurry off. But my duties here at the estate are arduous. I have little time to myself." With a warm goodbye for them both he made his exit.

When Jeffrey had closed the door on him and waited long enough for him to walk away he looked at her with a delighted smile. "We fooled him," he said. "He believes every word of our story."

"You're mad!" she cried in despair. "Couldn't you tell that he was making fun of you? Leading you on like some imbecile! He knows why we have come and he means to make us pay dearly for it!"

"I disagree!"

"You always disagree," she said bitterly. "We'll never leave here alive!"

"Now you're being melodramatic," her brother told her. "This is the United States. He can't get away with his sly tricks and black magic here!"

"I'm not really so sure of that!" she said.

Jeffrey looked baffled. "If you'd only have more confidence in me!"

"I'm sorry but I haven't!" she said unhappily.

And then she rushed by him, ignoring his dismayed expression and went out the front door into the warm sunshine of the morning. She turned to walk to the path along the cliffs only to be confronted by a figure so weird she involuntarily let out a cry of alarm. It was a woman, shabbily dressed, all in black, and wearing a black, heavy veil over her head and shoulders so her features were completely hidden!

CHAPTER 6

The bizarre female seemed startled by Anita's arrival. After a brief moment, the woman turned and hurried away from her in the direction of the great sprawling mansion of Collinwood. Anita stood watching the retreating figure and wondering who she was and what she was doing there. She also had a feeling that it was this strange creature she'd seen peering in through the window of her bedroom the previous night.

The woman in black vanished around a corner of the imposing structure of Collinwood. Anita sighed and then resumed her walk towards the path that followed the cliffs. She could see the village of Collinsport on a point of distant land on the right and directly opposite it on a smaller point was the Collinsport lighthouse. The curving bay between these distant peninsulas faced the estate.

As she drew near the edge of the cliff she saw that it was a dizzying drop to the beach below. The crash of the waves indicated an incoming tide and the sharp smell of the salt water was invigorating. It was truly a beautiful spot but was all this beauty merely a setting for evil? She was convinced that her brother had been wrong in his search for revenge and in coming to this isolated place. But she knew he was far too stubborn to change his tactics now that he had come to Collinwood.

Quentin had been crafty in his performance but she felt

he was still the figure of evil he had been in Venice. She had been deceived by him for a short time then but she felt this would never happen again. She could never again give him her trust.

She passed the main house of Collinwood scarcely noticing it because of her absorption with these thoughts. She was continuing on towards the high point of the cliffs when she saw another odd figure coming towards her. This time it was a man. An elderly man leaning heavily on a cane as he limped along.

She halted on the path as the elderly man came close to her. He had a bronzed, gnarled face and wore a red hunting cap and a heavy jacket in the same shade over gray trousers even though it was a fairly warm morning. The odd-looking man showed no surprise at seeing her but paused to give her a shrewd scrutiny from narrowed eyes.

"You one of the new people?" he asked in a rasping voice.

"Yes," she said.

He continued to stare at her. "I'm Jasper Collins, uncle to Quentin. I guess he brought you here?"

"No," she said. "My brother rented the cottage from the estate lawyer."

"I didn't hear about that," Jasper Collins said, leaning on his cane as he studied her. "I took it for granted you were another one of his women friends."

She frowned. "I don't understand."

The old man gave a sharp, curt laugh. "He's got the house full of them. That widow who never takes off her veil, supposed to be here for her health. According to him her husband died a little while ago and was his best friend. So he's trying to help her. And then there's Laura Cranston staying here. She was a friend of my daughter's and came to visit her but she's staying on at Quentin's invitation. And now she doesn't seem to have time for anyone else."

"You make this Quentin sound irresistible to women."

The old man showed disgust. "My own daughter, Georgina, who should have rightly inherited Collinwood, was shunted aside because she's adopted. The will did give us the privilege of staying on here as long as we liked. I would have packed and left the minute Quentin got here but for her. She thinks he's wonderful and is staying on as a sort of glorified housekeeper!"

"You don't approve?"

"I don't approve of anything about him," the old man snapped. "On top of everything else he brought along one of them Italian girls to take charge of the house. Name of Mirabelle, she don't speak proper English and hardly any of the help knows what she's talking about half the time. So Georgina does most of her work for free. But that's the way Quentin likes things. He enjoys having power over people. Keeping them at his beck and call."

"I'm sure he doesn't do that to you."

The old man chortled. "No question about that. I tell him what I think whether he likes it or not. And he can't put me out because of the will. Did you know his older brother? The one who died?"

"No," she said.

"He was all right though I don't approve of the will he made," Jasper Collins grumbled. "But this Quentin was never more than a playboy. I knew we would have trouble as soon as he came back."

"And have you?"

"It's not a pleasant place any more," the old man said solemnly. "And he's turned Georgina against me to the point where she always takes his side. It's the same with all those women in the house. They think the sun shines on Quentin. Even the crazy one in the veil who never talks. You can tell it in her ways."

"He does have a strange magnetism," she agreed.

"The Devil at work in him," Jasper Collins snapped. "That's what it is. Collinwood has always been a place of haunts and ghosts and the like. But we never had any Devil worshipers here until now." The old eyes under the narrowed lids searched her face. "You seem like a sensible enough young woman. You take my advice and stay clear of him."

"I'll do my best," she said, hardly knowing how to answer.

At that moment the old man's expression changed. He looked uneasily over her shoulder. Anita heard light footsteps approaching and turned to see an attractive blonde girl in a long brown skirt and a blouse with a high neck and bow in the front.

The girl looked angry as she marched across the lawn to join them. When she came close she addressed herself directly to the old man, saying, "I hope you haven't been subjecting this poor girl to one of your long tirades, Father."

Jasper Collins looked unhappy. "Of course not," he protested. "We were just exchanging the time of day."

"It took you long enough to do it," the girl said.

"I was just on my way back to the house," Jasper said unhappily. Indicating Anita with a nod, he said, "This is the girl from the cottage. They got here last night."

The blonde girl turned to her and held out her hand in an almost mannish fashion, "I'm Georgina Collins," she said. "And from what Quentin tells me you are Anita Burgess."

"Yes," she said, accepting the firm hand of the old man's daughter as he ambled off guiltily, leaving them alone.

Georgina seemed to be appraising her. "Our lawyer told us your name was Carson. But that seems to have been an error on his part."

"A misunderstanding," Anita said.

The other girl smiled coldly. "They happen. I hope you'll enjoy your holiday here."

"It's a lovely spot," she said, glancing at the bay.

"It can be, depending on the weather," Georgina said. "I hope my father didn't bore you with a lot of nonsense."

Anita could sense the curiosity and uneasiness behind the girl's words. It was clear she didn't trust her father's discretion. She said, "He's a most interesting person."

Georgina showed a wariness. "He rambles a lot. And not much of what he says can be counted on as truth."

"Oh?" She pretended polite surprise.

"You may think that an odd way for me to speak of my father," Georgina said. "But I feel frankness is required. He had a stroke a few years ago as you can see by his limp. It left his mind somewhat impaired."

"He seemed logical enough in his conversation with me."

"Because you don't know him well enough," the blonde girl said evenly. "He was no doubt wandering but you weren't aware of it. You'll be exposed to him while you're renting the cottage so it's only fair to tell you."

"Thanks. I'm sure he won't be a bother."

"He can be if he takes it in his head," the other girl sighed. "You have no idea how unreasonable he is at times. One of the unfortunate results of his illness has been his violent likes and dislikes. There is no sense in this. As an example, he has taken a dislike to Quentin Collins, who is a fine man. But don't try to tell that to my father."

Anita forced a smile. "The old are often strange in their attitudes."

"I'm trying to tell you my father is slightly insane," Georgina said curtly. "I guess it's best to come right out with it."

"I'm sorry," she said.

Georgina shrugged and turned to watch the distant figure of her father as he moved slowly towards Collinwood. "I have learned to cope with him. It hasn't been easy." She paused and then changing the subject said, "You met Quentin in Europe, I understand."

"Yes. In Venice."

"I believe he was very happy there," Georgina said. "It is a shame he had to return here and take the responsibility for Collinwood."

"He appeared satisfied when I spoke to him this morning," she said. "It could be the change will be good for him."

"Perhaps," she said. "We'll be seeing you and your brother at dinner."

"Yes," Anita said. "We really should have waited for a little before accepting Quentin's invitation. We don't want to be a nuisance."

"There's no bother," Georgina said. "Quentin is anxious to have you see the house and meet the others."

"I'm sure my brother, Jeffrey, is looking forward to it," she said. "I thought I'd walk as far as that high point of the cliffs."

Georgina glanced ahead. "Widow's Hill," she said. "There are many legends associated with it."

"Really?"

"You'll hear about them if you remain here long enough," the girl said. "The people in these small Maine villages are still a very superstitious lot."

"You must understand them very well."

"Not as well as I could," Georgina said. "My father and I have only been living here a few years. Before that we made our home in Boston. I must get back to the house. Enjoy your walk."

The blonde girl left her and she went on to the jutting high point of the cliffs. There was a bench there and she sat on it in the pleasant warmth of the sun and reviewed her recent conversation. She put little stock in the story that Jasper Collins was demented. Georgina had said that merely to cover up for any indiscreet remark made by her father. The old man was eccentric, but not crazy.

And he had surely told the truth of his daughter's domination by the suave Quentin. Anita had been aware of her same blind devotion to the dubious young man that the lovely girls of his cult in Venice had shown. Georgina was clearly on Quentin's side whether he be right or wrong. Even when, according to her father's version of things, Quentin had stepped in to inherit the property she'd hoped would be hers.

She frowned as she began to see that the pattern of living at Collinwood must be taking on much the same tone as that of Quentin's palace in Venice. He had once again started to surround himself with a group of lovely young women whom he could dominate. She'd been especially interested in the old man's mention that Quentin had brought a housekeeper with him from Italy, a girl named Mirabelle. Surely she must be one of the original cultists!

Then there was that mystery figure in the black dress and veil. Not even Jasper Collins appeared to know much about her. The way she acted at once made her a suspicious character. Everything Anita had learned thus far boded ill for Jeffrey's plan of revenge. With this summing up of things, she left the bench to start the fairly long walk back to the cottage.

Most of the day she spent taking care of their clothes and

arranging the cottage to their convenience. She was busy hanging some things in her closet in the late afternoon when she heard a carriage halt outside the front door. Jeffrey had left with the announcement that he was going down to inspect the small wharf, so she was alone.

She went out to the living room and opened the entrance door of the cottage to see the young lawyer they'd met on the boat stepping out of a small carriage. Seeing her he smiled.

"I've come to see you sooner than I expected," he said.

"You're very welcome," she told him.

"I'll tie up the horse," he said. "Then I have something to tell you." He led the horse and carriage over to an elm tree to the right of the cottage and tied the animal there.

Anita watched and it struck her there was an air of urgency in his manner. As he came back to her she saw he had a serious expression on his face. She stood back for him to enter the cottage.

"Can I get you some refreshment?" she asked.

He raised a protesting hand. "No, thank you. I can't stay too long. But I was worried about you and wanted to see how you were managing."

"Not badly so far," she said.

"Have you met some of the people here?"

"Quite a few of them," she said. "Quentin Collins called here this morning. And I've talked to his Uncle Jasper and also to his cousin, Georgina."

David Benson showed interest. "Does it strike you there's anything strange about the place?"

It was a surprising question. She stared at him. "What exactly do you mean?"

"I wondered if any of those you met or anything that has happened might have struck you as odd?"

She frowned slightly. "I think there is a good deal of tension here."

"Please go on."

"And I have met one weirdly dressed woman. She is supposed to be a widow and friend of Quentin. She dresses all in black and has a heavy black veil draped over her head and shoulders so you can see nothing of her face."

The young lawyer said, "That sounds strange enough."

"Why have you asked me this question?"

They were seated on a shabby love seat in the cottage living room. He shifted his weight to look directly at her with a worried air. "Because I have been hearing some upsetting rumors in the village."

"I'm not surprised. I hear the people in the area are superstitious."

"It is possible they have reason to be," he said grimly.

"Please go on."

"At least some of the stories going around were started by a village girl who was employed at Collinwood as a maid. When Quentin arrived he brought some Italian girl with him and made her housekeeper."

"I think her name is Mirabelle. I haven't met her."

"According to the maid, this Italian girl is a rather formidable type. The local girl became aware of certain mysterious goings-on in the house after the arrival of Quentin. For one thing he at once reserved one of the rooms on an upper floor for some kind of meetings."

"Meetings?"

"Yes," the young lawyer said seriously. "This ex-maid claims that every evening Quentin and several of the young women in the house gathered in that room which he had refurnished. She managed to get a key to the room from the housekeeper's ring and went up one night after the meeting had ended. She found the place to be completely draped in black with a small table at the end of it on which a human skull rested."

Anita gasped. "I have seen a room like that before!"

"Where?"

"In Venice," she said, without going into details since David Benson knew nothing of her acquaintanceship with Quentin over there.

The young man's face was shadowed. "The girl claimed there was also a smell of incense in the room and a burner for that purpose by the table with the skull. She also found a half-dozen black robes draped over some plain chairs."

"It sounds like a kind of cult," she said.

"Yes. Unfortunately for the girl, Quentin found her in the room."

"Oh? What was his reaction?"

"At first he upbraided her for being in the room and then took a softer tone. He said that he was fitting it out as a medieval place for meditation. He explained that he and the others were searching for peace of mind. And he invited the girl to take part in their rituals."

"What was her reaction?"

"She was terrified because she was convinced that Quentin and his followers had set apart the room for the worship of the Devil. She asked him what she would be required to do at the rituals. He wasn't too clear. But from what he said the girl got the impression she was supposed to help at the weird altar with the human skull on it. The idea was revolting to her and she refused. Quentin became angry and told her that because of her narrow-mindedness and spying she wasn't wanted at Collinwood any longer."

"And so he let her go?"

"Yes. She was too afraid to talk at first. Certain they would place an evil spell on her. But gradually she's gained confidence and repeated her story for others in the village. You can guess what a sensation it has caused. The facts becoming more graphic as the gossips elaborate on them."

"I'm sure I can," she agreed. "It was very stupid of Quentin to tell her so much and then discharge her."

"Without question," the young lawyer said. "This girl had great respect for Georgina Collins before Quentin came. Now she says that Georgina is under his spell and her whole personality has changed."

"My impression was that she's loyal to Quentin."

"No doubt of that," he said. "The girl claims the one person she trusted at Collinwood was Georgina's father, Jasper Collins. And he and Quentin don't get along."

"I gathered that," she said.

"The villagers say Collinwood has become a black magic headquarters and Quentin is using the young women around him as his pawns. That is why I rushed out here to warn you of the danger you could be in."

She gave him a grateful smile. "That was good of you. The truth is I wasn't unaware there might be danger here. Both my brother and I met Quentin in Italy. We have an idea of the extent to which his character has been twisted."

"Then you agree he is a menace?"

"I'm sure of it."

David Benson frowned. "Then why did you come here? You're exposing yourself to possible grave danger!"

She sighed. "It is my brother's idea. From his standpoint there are good reasons. Because he has confided in me I can't tell you everything at this time."

David Benson seemed worried. "I hope you will soon take me into your full confidence. If what that girl says is true, and it likely is, who knows what kind of dreadful things are going on here?"

"I agree," she said. "I'll speak to Jeffrey and tell him what you've been kind enough to tell me."

"I wish you would," the young man said, rising. "It is just possible Quentin is enslaving these young women by giving them drugs or even through hypnotism."

"His eyes do have a strange power in them."

David was standing facing her. "I don't want to wait until you are one of his victims."

"There's not much danger of that happening," she said. "I'm aware of what he's doing."

"I hope so," David worried. "But even the slight knowledge I have of him suggests that he's entirely unscrupulous. And there are some more alarming stories being told about him."

"More alarming?"

"In a way it ties in with the Satan worshiping story," he said. "But now there are whispers Quentin is a werewolf."

Again she thought of Venice. The identical stories had been going the rounds there. Surely there must be some basis for them.

She said, "What makes them say that?"

"Since Quentin has returned to Collinwood, a number of people have seen a ghostly wolf. It appears usually under a full moon and in isolated fields or such places. But once it was reported on the edge of the village."

"Do you believe these accounts?"

The young lawyer looked baffled. "I never have before. But as I've listened to the various people who are supposed to have seen the creature I'm beginning to wonder. They give such a complete description of the animal."

"And they all agree on its appearance?"

"Yes. It apparently shows as greenish-gray under the moon. It has shining amber eyes and a blood curdling howl."

She gave a tiny shudder. "That's a vivid enough picture."

"To make it all seem more likely," David Benson said, "there have been two bodies found in the same period. Both with their throats ripped open. The local people say it was the werewolf. And that the werewolf is Quentin."

She said, "You've given me good reason to fear this place."

"I think you should leave."

"I'll speak to my brother," she said, rising.

"Would it do any good if I talked to him? Warned him of the hazards of having you remain here?"

She shook her head. "You don't understand him. Or his reasons for coming to Collinwood. I think the matter can be best handled by me."

The young lawyer appeared reluctant to leave it at this. He moved slowly to the door and then turned to say, "If you can get him to change his mind about staying you are welcome to come to my parents' home as guests. We have the room and would be glad to have you. And you'd be far enough away from Collinwood that you'd be relatively safe."

She smiled. "That's a generous offer. I'll tell my brother about it."

David Benson stared at her with concern. "In our short

acquaintance I've come to be very fond of you," he said.

"You are too kind."

"No," he insisted. "It is my wish that we might become better friends. So this is now a personal problem for me."

"Thank you, David," she said.

"I'm going to worry about you as long as you're here."

"I'm sorry."

He came close to her, concern strong in his eyes. "You must be very careful. Promise me."

"I will," she said gently.

Then David took her in his arms a moment and kissed her. It was a warm, tender kiss and came as a complete surprise. She made no effort to resist it and after a moment he let her go.

"Do you hate me for that?" he asked.

She sighed. "No. But I perhaps wish it hadn't happened."

"Why?"

"The closer we become, the greater the strain on you. You will be that much more concerned about my welfare."

He smiled faintly. "Is that your only objection?"

"Yes."

He touched her arm. "Then it doesn't matter. My degree of concern is bound to be great in any case."

"Come back again," she said.

"Be sure of that," David told her. "And if your brother should be willing to leave here before I do return, don't hesitate to come directly to my home. Anyone in the village can tell you where it is."

"I'll remember," she smiled.

She saw him out to the carriage and then remained outside the cottage until he had driven off. Turning to go back inside, she happened to look in the direction of Collinwood. And she saw what looked like Quentin standing on its front steps watching her. She hurried in out of sight with a chill of fear shooting through her.

The stories she'd just heard from David Benson filled her with fresh terror. If all that he had said were true, then things were as bad at Collinwood as they had been in Venice. Quentin Collins in returning had brought his evil with him. But wasn't that to be expected?

Knowing that Quentin had seen the young lawyer visiting her gave her additional cause for alarm. The memory of what had happened to that other young man who'd loved her was all too fresh in her mind. She was sure that Quentin had callously arranged the death of Arnold Tenn. If he suspected that she and David were falling in love, he'd soon find a way to eliminate him.

It worried her that she wasn't able to tell David about all that had happened in Venice. In that way she would be able to give him a hint of the danger he risked in paying attention to her. But her first loyalty had to be to Jeffrey. Until she had permission from him she would have to be discreetly silent about many things.

Jeffrey returned to the cottage about a half-hour later. He seemed weary and he reminded her of their dinner appointment at Collinwood around seven. She, in turn, told him of David Benson's visit. She watched her brother's reaction as he listened to the stories.

When she'd finished he gave her a troubled glance. "At least what he told you proves me right in my contention that Quentin hasn't reformed."

"I know."

Her brother's face was shadowed. "And it makes it all the more urgent that I do something to destroy him."

"If you are able."

"I'll find a way," he said confidently.

"I wasn't too surprised about the fact he's setting up another black magic cult here," she said. "That was to be expected. But the werewolf thing is shocking."

Her brother gave her a strange glance. "And probably true!"

She opened her eyes wide. She hadn't expected him to say this. She said, "Why do you think so?"

He took a deep breath. "When I was down on the beach just now I saw some animal tracks above the water line. Weird tracks! Larger than would be made by any dog or animal native to the area."

CHAPTER 7

At seven o'clock Quentin greeted them at the entrance to Collinwood. He was wearing a dark suit and black string tie, and looked the model of a respectable country squire. As he shook hands with Jeffrey and gave her a smiling greeting, Anita couldn't help wondering at his deceit and speculate about that locked room upstairs.

"We will be joining the others in a moment," Quentin said. "Among them you'll meet Eleanor Kent. You must not be made uneasy by her. She was recently widowed and insists on wearing a dark veil and mourning clothes. It is an eccentricity but because her husband was a close friend I'm trying to indulge her and help her through this difficult period."

"I have already met her. She was walking by the cottage and when she saw me she ran off," Anita told him.

He nodded. "Then you will be better prepared for her. She will likely do no more than nod to your greeting and don't expect her to take any part in a conversation. She is in a deep depression."

Jeffrey raised his eyebrows. "Wouldn't she be better under a doctor's care than here?"

"Several doctors have seen her and not been able to help. I felt it my duty to try and save her from a lunatic asylum," Quentin said.

Anita thought about the black-draped room and the masses to Satan and felt that being here in this eerie atmosphere could easily drive the woman mad. It was probably the worst possible place for her.

She said, "Do you feel it a fearful responsibility?"

Their host eyed her mockingly. "I'm used to burdens of the sort," he said. "Now you must come into the living room and meet everyone."

Georgina, coolly regal in a sweeping white gown, was the first to greet them. Then they met the veiled woman, who bore out Quentin's prediction by merely nodding to them.

Jasper Collins sat glumly near the veiled woman and was the next one they met. He gazed up at them and said, "I envy you both. The cottage is the best place to live. This house isn't the same any more!"

Quentin passed this off with a laugh. "My uncle is one of those people who only enjoy looking backward. The past is always preferable to the present!"

"It is here!" Jasper said, leaning his hands on his cane head and glaring at him defiantly.

Quentin led them on to a willowy, rather lovely dark-haired girl. "This is Laura Cranston," he said. "She was a schoolmate of Georgina's and is visiting here with us for an indefinite stay."

Anita smiled at the girl. "You must be fond of Maine."

"I am," Laura Cranston said. "It is so much cooler here than in the city. I hope I may stay at least until the end of summer."

Anita noticed that her brother and Quentin had gone over to talk with Georgina. Alone with the Cranston girl she decided to try and find out something about her. According to Georgina's father the girl had completely lost her head to Quentin.

Anita said, "What a sad creature that poor widow is."

Laura nodded. "I agree. It is only because of Quentin's generous heart that he allows her to remain."

"You admire Quentin a good deal, I take it," she said staring at the girl.

The dark girl blushed. "I consider him a fine man."

"And well-traveled," Anita said. "Has he told you about his palace in Venice?"

"No."

"You should get him to describe it to you one day. And mention his adventures there."

A gleam of jealousy showed in Laura's eyes proving to Anita that Laura Cranston was indeed infatuated with the wily Quentin. The dark girl said, "You seem to know a great deal about him."

"Not really. Though I did encounter him once in Italy."

"I have never been abroad," Laura Cranston said in a tone that suggested she felt cheated.

"No doubt you will one day," she said. "It is best to go in the company of somebody who has made the journey before and then they can help you find the interesting places."

Laura's face brightened. "When I do go that is what I plan to do."

Again this confirmed Anita's suspicions. No doubt Quentin had been filling the girl with promises of taking her abroad. He would be capable of telling Georgina the same lies. It was one of his ways of getting their loyalty while he was loyal to no one.

Glancing around the elegantly furnished living room with its huge crystal chandeliers, she said, "What a lovely house it is! And so large! I suppose you've been all through it."

"Most of it," Laura Cranston said. "A few of the rooms are shut off."

"There would be no use for them," she suggested.

"Not now," the other girl said. "The house was built a number of years after the old house. Jeremiah Collins was the first one of the Collins family to settle here. And he completed the old house in 1795."

"That would be the house Barnabas Collins occupies," Anita said.

"Yes." An odd look had come to Laura's attractive face.

"I saw him briefly at the wharf when we arrived last night," she said.

"Oh?"

"And again a little later. He was walking along the side of the road in the darkness. He seemed lost in his thoughts."

"He is a recluse," Laura Cranston said with a slight suggestion of scorn.

"I hadn't heard that."

"He stays at the old house with a single servant," the other girl said. "And he never leaves it during the daytime."

"That's odd."

"He's odd in other ways," Laura said bitterly. "He makes few friends and he does all he can to embarrass Quentin."

"Why?"

"Apparently he doesn't think Quentin should have inherited Collinwood," the girl said. "And I don't know anyone else who would manage the estate in better fashion."

"Perhaps he fears that Quentin won't remain here," she said. "After all, he has been a wanderer. It must be hard for him to settle down."

"I think the responsibility of the estate has made him want to remain in one place," Laura said. She glanced across the room where Georgina was standing with Quentin and Jeffrey. "Georgina would have been in line for Collinwood if his older brother hadn't left it to Quentin. And that would hardly be fair since she is only an adopted Collins."

"How does she feel about it?"

"She's not upset. She adores Quentin as we all do. But her father has been impossible," the girl said, glaring at old Jasper, who sat in grim majesty by the side of the veiled woman. "He feels his adopted daughter had an equal right with Quentin, which is not reasonable. Because of his own uncertain temperament he'd been eliminated years ago as a possible heir."

"At least they have the privilege of always living here."

Laura gave her a startled glance. "How did you happen to know that?"

"I had a brief chat with Jasper Collins this morning."

"You seem to have met nearly everyone."

"I suppose I have now," she said.

Laura frowned. "I don't think it is right that Quentin should always have to let Georgina and her dreadful old father live with him!"

"But it was stipulated in his brother's will, wasn't it?"

"Then his brother didn't use good judgment," was Laura's angry comment. "I don't think Quentin would mind Georgina being here. But her father is a different matter!"

Anita asked, "Does Barnabas Collins visit here?"

"When he feels like it," she said with some annoyance. "I think he comes just to see what is going on. To keep tabs on Quentin. He doesn't like Quentin but he pretends to."

"How can you tell that?"

"Quentin warned me about him. He said to be careful of anything I told him. And I have been."

"I'm surprised," Anita said. "From his appearance I'd not suspect that Barnabas was sneaky in any way."

"Are you sure the man you saw was Barnabas?"

"I think so, from all the descriptions I've heard."

Laura said, "Come out to the reception hall a moment. I'll show you his portrait. You should be able to recognize him from it."

Anita followed the girl out to the hallway. And reaching there Laura halted before a portrait hung there which Anita hadn't noticed on her arrival. It was a fine painting of Barnabas in oils. Staring up at it in admiration, she said, "That's a striking likeness. And he is the same man I saw."

"You are wrong," the dark girl said with a satisfied smile. She was enjoying correcting her in this.

Anita stared at her. "What do you mean?"

"This isn't a painting of Barnabas but of an ancestor of his who lived here long ago."

"They're incredibly alike!"

"Yes. But the Barnabas in this portrait left Collinwood more than a century ago."

She gave Laura a thin smile. "You're well informed on the family history."

"I've read some books in the library and Quentin has told me a lot."

"He can be interesting when he likes," Anita admitted. "It is too bad he and his cousin don't get along better. I mean he and Barnabas."

"It has to be Barnabas's fault," Laura said airily.

"Yes, I suppose so," she agreed. For she could tell that as far as Laura was concerned Quentin was faultless.

This was the kind of hero worship always found in his followers. They went back inside to join the others.

Dinner was served in the dining room of Collinwood. As they were seated at the table she again had an unhappy recollection of that dining room in the palace in Venice. It had been dark except for the glowing candles on its table, and so was this room. The veiled woman sat across from her, and she began to have the uneasy feeling that her carriage and general outline reminded her of someone.

Jeffrey led a lot of the conversation at dinner. She could tell that her brother was in a reckless, excited mood and she hoped that he would not betray his true feelings towards their host. If he did he would find no friends with the exception of old Jasper Collins.

All at once her brother addressed himself to Quentin saying, "I hear there have been two rather mysterious murders in the area lately."

Quentin met the statement with unwavering calm. "I believe so. I don't take much interest in such violence. I busy myself with the affairs of the estate."

"But these crimes are your business, wouldn't you say?" Jeffrey taunted him. "You are responsible for the people on the estate."

"If you put it that way," Quentin said.

"I hear these unfortunate victims had their throats ripped as if by an animal," Jeffrey went on. Anita knew he was deliberately baiting Quentin and listened nervously to hear what the result might be.

Old Jasper Collins surprised her by speaking up loudly. "A werewolf!" he exclaimed.

This caused a mild sensation at the table. Georgina gave him a look of reproof. "We can do without your wild fantasies, Father!"

He glared at her indignantly. "That's not what I say. It's what all of Collinsport is saying!"

Having caused the situation, Jeffrey now slyly went on to develop it. He gave his attention to the old man, asking, "Just what do you mean, Mr. Collins?"

"Yes," Quentin said in a hard voice. "By all means explain yourself, Uncle Jasper. That is, if you can!" There was derision in his tone.

Georgina's father pointed a bony finger at him. "You needn't tell me this is the first time you've heard there was a werewolf around here!"

Quentin's face was crimson. "I explained that I pay no attention to ignorant gossip."

"People have seen the werewolf!" the old man cried. "And I have seen it on many a moonlight night here on the lawn and on the beach!"

Anita's eyes met her brother's and she saw the look of pleased satisfaction in them. He had gained something with his probing in the dark. His suspicions about the tracks on the beach were being confirmed by the old man.

There was an awkward silence at the table for a moment and then the cold Georgina smiled nastily at her father. "Of course you've seen the werewolf," she said. "You've seen a great many odd things. But only since you suffered your stroke!"

Jasper Collins gasped. "I never thought to live to be called crazy by my own daughter!"

"I'm only trying to prevent you from making yourself ridiculous, Father," she said calmly.

Quentin said, "I think the subject of werewolves should be dropped as a topic of dinner conversation. I find it boring and unlikely."

"I can understand your feelings," Jeffrey said in a parting shot. And the conversation did turn to something else.

But Anita feared that Jeffrey had revealed himself much too openly. Especially in his last biting comment. She thought she had seen a certain look in Quentin's eyes at the time. A look of sheer hatred!

With dinner ended they all filed back into the living room again. Anita found herself alone with Quentin at the end of the room nearest the reception hall.

He studied her with admiring eyes. "All during dinner I was thinking how lovely you are."

She gave him a knowing look. "You have continually surrounded yourself with such lovely young women that I'm sure feminine beauty is no novelty to you."

"That is not true. I find you unique. But I fear your brother still has no liking for me."

She quickly went to Jeffrey's defense. "But that can't be true. Otherwise he wouldn't have sought you out and come here to apologize for his actions in Venice."

Quentin's hypnotic eyes fixed on hers. "Do you really believe that is why he came here?"

She tried to sound very casual. "There could be no other reason."

"There might be," he said very evenly. "Revenge."

She pretended to be startled by this. "You are wrong. If that were so he wouldn't have brought me along."

Quentin smiled oddly. "Perhaps he saw you as an accomplice?"

She knew she had to make a brazen attempt at a bluff. "Do you think that possible?" She was counting on his pride to defeat his astuteness.

He hesitated, then he said, "No."

"Thank you," she told him quietly.

"You're still a mystery to me," he went on to say.

"Isn't that good?"

"In a way," he agreed. "I hope that this time we don't part in the same way we did before."

"The circumstances are much different now."

"You lost Arnold and I lost Mara," Quentin said. "It should have brought us together. Yet you preferred to place all the blame on me and let it tear us apart."

"I've grown wiser," she said.

"I think you have," Quentin said, staring at her.

To avoid his eyes she glanced out in the direction of the shadowed reception hall and suddenly saw the figure of a woman standing there watching them. A young woman in the dark dress and white apron and cap of a servant. Most startling of all, her face was familiar. Anita was sure she had seen her in that palace of Quentin's in Venice. The woman appeared frightened and vanished in the shadows.

Quentin asked, "What is it? You seem shocked by something." He turned and glanced out at the hallway where the girl had been a few seconds before.

"Nothing," she said. "Just something that crossed my mind."

"It couldn't have been anything pleasant," Quentin said. "Do you care to confide in me?"

She smiled at him. "I think you'd better go and give some time to Laura Cranston. She's standing by the fireplace glaring at me." It was true the dark girl was showing unmistakable signs of jealousy.

He glanced carelessly in her direction and then told Anita, "Perhaps I should talk to her. I'll be back shortly."

Anita was relieved to have him go. She had come to hate and distrust him. The strain of pretending to have forgiven him was almost too much for her. She didn't manage it nearly as well as Jeffrey. She saw that her brother was in conversation with Georgina and guessed that he was trying to get what information he could from her.

The woman in the black veil had vanished and old Jasper Collins sat by himself in a high-backed chair staring straight ahead of him with a look of annoyance on his face. Feeling compassion for the beleaguered old man she went over to him.

"I enjoyed our talk this morning," she said.

He looked up at her with a hurt expression. "Everyone around here thinks I'm crazy!"

"You mustn't think that," she told him.

"My daughter does. You heard her at the table."

"I'm sure she didn't mean it."

"She meant it well enough. That girl has no proper respect for me. And I lavished nothing but affection on that girl since the day we adopted her. You never can tell how they'll turn out."

She wanted to change the subject so she said, "I was interested in what you said about a werewolf. Did you really see it?"

"More than once!" He gave her a triumphant look. "You know what they're saying in the village, don't you?"

"We only just got here."

He leaned forward and in a low tone informed her, "They're saying Quentin is the werewolf! They say it because that maid he let go told around he's practicing black magic here."

"Do you think it could be true?"

"Wouldn't surprise me," he said, sinking back in the chair. "Nothin' like that ever happened here until he turned up."

The old man seemed disinterested in talking any more. He sat there content with his malevolent thoughts about the hated Quentin. She had no desire to join in a conversation with any of the others so she moved down to the doorway leading to the hall and went out to stand before the painting of the ancestor of Barnabas Collins.

Even in the shadows she found the likeness to the man she'd seen the previous night startling. The same stern yet handsome face, the same deep-set understanding eyes that had made the man on the wharf remain vivid in her memory.

There was a slight sound of someone moving behind her and then a low pleasant voice asked, "Do you admire that painting?"

She turned in surprise to find herself looking up at Barnabas Collins. The tall man in the caped coat was smiling at her. She said, "I didn't hear you come in."

"I entered by the back door," he said. "I sometimes do. I dislike formal entrances, especially when my cousin has guests."

"I understand this is a painting of an ancestor of yours," she said. "It looks so much like you."

"I agree," he said, looking up at the painting. "I wonder that Quentin allows it to hang there since he is not one of my admirers."

She smiled at him. "I've heard so much about you. I've wanted to meet you."

His deep-set eyes showed a twinkle. "I thought Quentin was the one who commanded all the feminine attention. I'm flattered."

"My name is Anita Burgess," she said. "My brother, Jeffrey, and I have rented the cottage for the summer."

"Of course," Barnabas said. "I heard you were arriving but I didn't know when."

"It's a beautiful spot," she said. "Your family must have spent a lot of time finding it."

"I keep returning here," he confessed. "There is no other place quite like it for me." He hesitated. "It's a lovely night outside. Why don't we carry on our conversation out there?"

"I'd like that," she said. "But I should let my brother know first."

Barnabas smiled. "If you go back in there to tell him you'll never get away."

"I suppose you're right," she said.

"Be reckless," Barnabas said, and he took her hand in his. She noticed that it was strangely cold but soon forgot it.

They quietly let themselves out the front door and she at once saw that he was right. It was a lovely night with a sky full of stars and not too cold. The air was fresh and stimulating and it was quiet except for the distant sound of the waves on the shore.

He suggested, "Let us walk towards Widows' Hill."

"I'd like that," she said. "I walked that far this morning."

As they strolled across the lawn, he said, "You say you have heard a great deal about me? From whom?"

"A number of people. The first time was in Venice."

"Venice?" he sounded surprised.

"Yes. My brother and I were there with someone else. We met Quentin, and several people of the American colony mentioned that you had been there but hadn't stayed long."

"That is so," he said in a dry voice.

"I suppose I shouldn't speak so frankly at our first meeting," she said. "But there were rumors that you didn't approve of your cousin, Quentin."

"I see."

"The gossip went that you had come for a stay in Venice but when you learned what was going on at the palace he'd taken over you decided to leave almost immediately."

Barnabas gave her a quizzical glance. "Did you think the rumors sounded reasonable?"

She looked up at him. "Knowing Quentin as I do. Yes."

"Then you are among that minority of young women who do not approve of my good-looking cousin?"

"I'm afraid I dislike him a great deal."

"Why?"

"I see through him as being something quite different from what he pretends," she said.

"Do you?" The tone of the man at her side was mocking.

"Yes."

"And your reason for this remarkable insight into my cousin's character?"

"He was responsible for the death of my fiance in Venice," she said bitterly, blurting out the truth she hadn't intended to reveal.

He halted and gazed down at her with deep sympathy showing on his handsome face. "I'm sorry," he said sincerely.

"It's all right," she said. There was a hint of a break in her voice as all the sadness about Arnold returned.

Barnabas Collins took her arm and guided her gently along in the direction of Widows' Hill. There was a silence between them as they walked under the stars. Then, after a little while, Barnabas said, "If it isn't too painful for you I wish you'd tell me the whole story."

"Why not?" she said. And she did.

It took quite a little while. They arrived at the high point of the cliffs and sat on the bench together as she finished her account of those tragic days in Venice.

Barnabas was studying her. "You have gone through an

ordeal. I don't think your brother had any right to bring you here."

"I was against coming."

"And quite understandably," he said.

She sighed. "But now that I am here I know I must remain. For one thing we've proof that Quentin is setting up another black magic circle. He is still the same evil man."

"I'm well aware of that," Barnabas said.

"And so it is important that something be done about him. That he be prevented from ruining other lives."

"He is a very cunning fellow," Barnabas warned her.

"My brother is a person of strong character," she said. "I'm sure he'll find a way to punish Quentin."

"Until then it is going to be a struggle between the forces of good and evil here," Barnabas said. "With you exposed to the attacks from either side."

Anita asked him, "If you dislike Quentin so much, why did you decide to come back here?"

His deep-set eyes met hers. "My purpose is somewhat like yours. I want to find a way to destroy him."

CHAPTER 8

B arnabas's solemn words gave her a feeling of encouragement.
She gazed up into his stern, handsome face. "Then my brother
and I are not alone in our mission?"

"Yes and no," he said. "I have to approach this in a rather
different way from you."

"He is already in serious trouble in the village. Those
two men were killed and gossip has it that he's the werewolf
responsible."

"I've heard that story," Barnabas said.

"I believe it," she told him. "Even in Venice there was talk
of some monstrous wolf being seen in the moonlight during the
time Quentin was there."

Barnabas revealed no reaction to this. "Collinwood has
always been a setting for ghost stories and legends of every kind.
One more doesn't surprise me."

"But I'm sure there is a sound basis for this legend," she
said.

"There is for all of them," he told her. "One of the first ghost
tales had to do with this very place where we're sitting. Widows'
Hill was where the wives of fishermen used to come and wait
to discover which of the men would return safely after a storm.
And it was said a ghostly figure, the Phantom Mariner, appeared

before the eyes of those whose husbands had been drowned. Every fisherman's wife feared the vision of the Phantom Mariner."

"An old estate like this is bound to be linked with stories of ghosts," she agreed.

"There was another legend associated with my own ancestor whose painting you admired such a short time ago," Barnabas said. "He was banished from Collinwood because he was supposed to have been cursed with the bite of a bat. The curse was placed on him by a jealous woman and the villagers believed he had become a vampire. One of the walking dead."

"The walking dead?" she echoed.

He nodded sadly. "Yes. One of those doomed to walk the earth for eternity. Allowed to show themselves only between dusk and dawn and forced to prey on the blood of other living humans to sustain their half-lives."

"How horrible!"

"I think so," he said quietly. "Those are only two of the phantom stories that have circulated about Collinwood. I could name a lot of others but it would have no purpose. Now we come to the werewolf legend and its link with Quentin."

"You sound as if you doubt he can transform himself into animal form?"

"I'm not ready to offer an instant judgment in the matter," Barnabas said. "But if it should be true, sooner or later he'll bring about his own downfall."

"I want to think that," she said.

Barnabas was staring at her with those deep-set eyes. "You must have loved that young man a good deal."

"I did," she said.

"Your bitterness reveals that now," he said. "Yet you have no actual evidence that Quentin directly caused his death."

"The girl did it. Quentin told her what to do. It was the same as if he had sent Arnold falling down those steep steps himself."

"True," Barnabas said. "You feel your brother has some plan to punish my cousin. Have you any idea what it may be?"

"No."

"Perhaps he is improvising, waiting for some opportunity to present itself now that he is here."

"It might be," she said. "Can I tell him you are on our side?"

Barnabas smiled grimly. "It might be better to say it differently. Tell him I will do all that I can to help him."

"I suppose that's the same thing," she said hesitantly. "When will I see you again? Can't you come visit us tomorrow at the cottage?"

"Not in the daytime," Barnabas said gently. "I never leave the house during the day."

She suddenly remembered. "Yes. I've heard about that. You're writing some kind of book and give it all the daylight hours. And you're supposed to be aloof and eccentric."

His smile was bleak. "Interesting adjectives."

"Well, it must be at least partly true," she said. "You don't talk to many people. You stay mostly by yourself."

"That is my preference."

"But why? You are such a charming man."

"Thank you," he said with amused irony. "But I'm not sure that everyone would agree with you in that."

"It's true," she persisted. "When I saw you standing in the shadows near the wharf last night watching the passengers come off the boat I thought you were one of the most distinguished-looking men I'd ever seen. If you had come closer and been friendly with the people I'm sure they would have liked you."

"Some of us are doomed to stand in the shadows."

She smiled at him. "Now you're being deliberately gloomy. It doesn't become you."

"I'm sorry," he said. "I'll try to do better."

"And you haven't said when we'll meet again or when I can have you meet Jeffrey?"

"Let us leave it open," he suggested. "If I can manage it I'll come by your cottage tomorrow evening."

"I'll expect you and I'll ask my brother to wait for your arrival."

"I may not be able to come," he warned her.

"I'll wait for you anyway," she said.

She was going to ask him some other questions but just then she saw a shadowy figure come striding along the path towards them. A feeling of apprehension shot through her and increased when she saw that it was Quentin Collins coming nearer them with an angry look on his side-whiskered face.

"It's Quentin!" she gasped as she stood up.

"Really?" Barnabas said, seeming not at all upset. He also got to his feet and turned to be ready for the approach of his cousin.

Quentin halted by them scowling. "So this is where you've been?"

"I trust this portion of the estate isn't denied to us," Barnabas said in a mocking manner. "Now that you control the place I'm never sure of what new rules you may make."

Quentin clenched his fists. "It wasn't a gentleman's act to sneak into the house and take this girl off with you!"

"You make an interesting point," Barnabas said.

"It was as much my fault as his," she protested. "I asked him to bring me out here."

Quentin coldly gave his attention to her. "You may be interested to know that your brother is very upset by your disappearance!"

"I didn't mean to worry him," she said.

"But you and my eccentric cousin have managed just that," Quentin said. "In fact Jeffrey practically accused me of doing you some harm before I left the house a few minutes ago."

"What a dreadful slander!" Barnabas smiled. "I don't know how he could think of you in such a villainous role."

Quentin seemed to be having trouble controlling his temper. He turned to her, "Since you've met my peculiar cousin and arrived at such friendly terms with him you should be willing to return to Collinwood now. Otherwise I can't promise what crazy conclusion your brother may come to."

"I suggest that you return ahead of us and convey the good news of Anita's safety to her brother," Barnabas said pleasantly. "We'll be following on your heels."

Quentin glared at him. Then he asked her, "Are you coming back with me?"

She felt it was a moment for a small defiance. Quentin had been having things his own way for much too long. So she said, "You go on. Barnabas and I will walk back together."

Quentin looked startled. Then he said grimly, "Very well. I hope you know what you are doing."

And with that he turned abruptly and started back in the direction of Collinwood.

She waited until he was out of earshot and then she smiled at Barnabas. "I hope we didn't make him too angry."

"No harm if we did," he said. "An angry man has less judgment. If we're to topple Quentin from his high place we've got to fight him in every way."

"We'd better go back," she said. "Jeffrey must be very upset. And he probably won't even believe Quentin when he tells him the truth."

"One of the disadvantages of being known as a consistent liar," Barnabas said, as they followed Quentin along the path.

"You two don't mind revealing how you feel about each other," she marveled.

"We have lived in this state of armed truce for much too long," Barnabas observed bleakly. "I'm wearying of it."

"You're so different from him," she said. "If you are eccentric it's a pleasant sort of eccentricity. You're not evil as he is."

"People may disagree with you on that," he warned her.

"They'll never make me change my mind," she promised.

Barnabas sighed. "This has been a perfect night for me. I doubt if one as good will come soon again."

"It's been wonderful meeting you," she said. "From now on I won't feel our mission is so hopeless."

They were within a short distance of the entrance to Collinwood and Barnabas halted. "I will leave you here," he said.

"You won't wait to meet my brother?"

"Not now," he said. "I have some other things to attend to."

She smiled up at him. "Don't forget about tomorrow night."

"I'll try and come by," he said. "And you take care." He patted her gently on the arm. "I'll stand here until you are safely inside."

And he did. She paused to wave at his solitary figure a distance away in the shadows and he waved back. Meeting him had changed things a great deal she felt. She went on inside with new courage.

Jeffrey was just on his way out of the living room to the reception hall. He looked worried and when he saw her he came over at once. "Where have you been?" he demanded.

"For a walk with Barnabas Collins. He's very nice."

Jeffrey frowned. "You should have told me. I was blaming Quentin and thinking any number of dreadful things might have happened to you."

"So he said."

"Don't ever do anything like that again," her brother warned her.

"You'll approve of Barnabas," she said. "He's coming by to talk to you at the cottage tomorrow evening."

Quentin emerged from the living room and came over to them. He gave her a bleak smile. "I see you decided to return."

"You knew I would," she said.

"You weren't in the best of company," Quentin said.

"I wouldn't say that," she told him.

Quentin glanced up at the portrait of Barnabas's ancestor. "You've probably heard that the original Barnabas left here under a cloud."

"Yes. He told me about it," she said.

Quentin gave her a taunting look. "Did he also mention that he has had similar problems?"

She frowned. "No."

"He should have," Quentin said smugly. "He ought to have been completely frank and explained the reason he doesn't live here permanently. And why he keeps to himself in the old house and is never seen in the days."

Jeffrey was showing interest in the young man's remarks. "Are you saying this Barnabas Collins isn't to be trusted?"

"Several times the gossip about him has made him leave here," Quentin said. "During his visits girls in the village and servants in the house here have been attacked. They were found wandering in a daze with a strange red mark on their throats. The local people called it the vampire's mark. Remembering the legend of the original Barnabas, they put the blame on my cousin."

"That was hardly fair," Anita said defiantly.

"Was he definitely linked with the attacks in any way?" her brother asked Quentin.

"Barnabas is very careful. He leaves the area whenever things get too pressing," Quentin said. "So he has avoided any real confrontation with the authorities."

"I'd say he was eccentric," Anita told the young man, "and I wouldn't go any further. Barnabas doesn't deny he is individual in his manner and way of living and he doesn't apologize for it."

"Believe the best of him if you like," Quentin said. "I'm sure in due time you'll understand him a lot better. Then you may remember what I've said just now."

"We must be going," Jeffrey said. "Thank you for the dinner and the opportunity of meeting your guests."

"It is something we must do often," Quentin said with one of his urbane smiles. He saw them to the door and on their way.

When they were a distance from the house Jeffrey turned to her and said, "From what he hinted this Barnabas is another twisted character. It would be wise to keep away from him."

"I don't believe that story," she protested.

"I don't think you should go out with him alone until we have at least made some further inquiries about him," her brother worried. "Maybe when David Benson visits us again he'll be able to give us new information on him." The mention of David made her feel less let-down.

Quentin's comments about Barnabas had made her uneasy. She still admired him but Quentin had been so emphatic in his hints that Barnabas was not all he pretended to be that it had shaken her confidence in him. At least David was one person she needn't worry about.

Now some new thoughts crowded into her mind as they walked the lonely path to the cottage. She said, "I didn't get a chance to mention it before. But while I was talking with Quentin I saw a young woman in servant's dress in the hallway watching all of us. And I'm sure I've seen her before. She was one of the girls belonging to his cult in Venice."

Her brother nodded. "That isn't surprising," he said. "Probably the girl you saw was the Mirabelle who Quentin brought with him when he came here."

"I'm sure of it," she said. "He's making Collinwood a headquarters for his Satanist activities just as he did with that castle in Venice."

"No question of it," Jeffrey worried. "Aside from old Jasper he has everyone under the spell of his charm."

"Certainly Georgina is on his side," she agreed. "And I'm sure that Laura Cranston has a crush on him."

"Foolish girls!" Jeffrey said bitterly. "But you can't warn them! They won't listen."

"I know something about that," she said ruefully.

"That's all in the past," he said. "You are wiser now." They arrived at the cottage and Jeffrey unlocked the door and they went inside. The lamp in the living room had been left burning and there were still some smouldering embers of the log fire in the fireplace. It was pleasantly cozy.

Anita sank down on the loveseat and said, "It was a strange evening. And you missed one of the most interesting parts of it when Quentin and Barnabas met. They hate each other and just barely manage to be civil."

"They're probably too much alike to get on well."

"No," she said. "Barnabas is much different from Quentin. I have faith in him no matter what others may say."

Jeffrey gave her a knowing look. "You've neglected mentioning one subject that interests me a lot."

"What?"

"You haven't given any opinion on the widow with her concealing veil."

She sighed. "What can I say about her? According to Quentin, her husband's death left her a mental case."

"A neat explanation," Jeffrey said. "It eliminates any need for her to talk or behave in a normal way. But I find it a little too glib a story."

Anita stared at him. "Why do you say that?"

"I have a theory about that veiled lady," Jeffrey said.

"Tell me."

"I think it is Mara," he said quietly.

"Mara!" she gasped.

"Why not?" he asked. "It could easily be. She's about the right size. And I've always doubted the girl they found in the canal with her throat cut was Mara."

Her eyes were wide with consternation. "I remember you

were skeptical about that," she agreed.

Jeffrey paced back and forth in front of the fireplace, caught up in the excitement of the idea. "What better disguise could she have? The veil covers her head completely and she never speaks so there's no chance to recognize her voice."

"It could be," she agreed.

"We've always felt Mara was his chief aide," Jeffrey went on. "I can't see him losing her so easily. I'd be willing to bet it was someone else's body the police found in Venice and Mara is living here at Collinwood as the veiled lady."

"The shadow at my window last night looked like her," Anita said. "It all fits in nicely."

"I think our veiled lady will bear close watching."

"If what you say turns out to be true she certainly will," Anita agreed.

"Quentin probably distrusts us," Jeffrey went on. "We've got to act really innocent until we've thrown him off guard."

"From what he said to me, I'd agree that you're right," she said. "I know Barnabas is willing to help us in any way he can."

"Let's reserve judgment on him until later," Jeffrey said. "And also let us get to bed at once. I'm completely exhausted."

It was fine again the next morning. At breakfast Jeffrey discussed the dinner party of the night before and again underlined his belief that the veiled woman was Mara in disguise. Anita listened with new interest each time he explained his reasons for thinking so. She was coming around to his point of view.

As they sat over coffee in the cheerful kitchen of the cottage, she asked him, "What happens next?"

His thin face shadowed. "I'm not quite sure."

"But you must have a plan," she said. "You can't have come here to extract vengeance from Quentin without at least some idea of what you mean to do."

"That is true," he agreed.

"I think you should tell me frankly what you have in mind and each step as the plan progresses. Otherwise how can I help you?"

Jeffrey gave her a reassuring glance. "You mustn't worry."

"But Barnabas was interested as well," she protested. "I'm sure we can count on his help if he knows what we want to do. How we count on paying Quentin back for his evil."

"I can't take Barnabas into my confidence at this point," Jeffrey warned her. "And I can't even give you an outline of how I wish to proceed for a few days."

"I feel so in the dark," she complained.

"You needn't," he said. "I'll come to you with the facts at the proper moment. Meanwhile you can help by keeping your eyes open and reporting anything unusual you see to me."

She sighed. "I worry that you may have no plan at all."

"I assure you I have," her brother said. "This morning I'm going in to Collinsport. I want to talk to a few people and find out certain things. I can probably get the use of a horse and carriage from the Collinwood stable."

And so he left the cottage early. Later he drove by in the carriage the Collinwood groom had given him and told her he'd not likely return until later in the day. She cleaned up after breakfast and then since it was another warm, sunny day decided to make another stroll of investigation of the rambling estate.

She walked along the cliff path but instead of heading for Widows' Hill changed direction when she came near the main house and went by it to pass the outbuildings and stables. She followed this path until the old Collinwood came into view, the one built by Jeremiah Collins in 1795 and in which Barnabas and his servant were staying now.

Barnabas had warned her not to try and get in touch with him during the day. But she hoped that in walking by his house she might catch a glimpse of him and be able to talk to him. She was anxious to tell him what Quentin had said about him and hear his reaction. She was sure Quentin had been talking out of turn but she wanted to hear Barnabas deny the allegations that had been made about him.

The plain red brick house was shuttered and deserted from outward appearance. But she knew Barnabas was in there somewhere. She didn't dare knock at the door. It might make Barnabas look on her as childish and inconsiderate. So she forced herself to move on to a broad field that slanted down to a thick forest a distance away. As she came to the rim of the hill she was startled to see a solitary black figure making her way to an iron-fenced cemetery that was located on the edge of the forest. It was the mysterious veiled lady!

At once Anita was curious. Why was the veiled woman going to the Collins family cemetery? Her late husband surely wouldn't be buried there. It could be her demented state that made her automatically seek out any cemetery as a place to contemplate in, or if this should be Mara in disguise there might be a much more prosaic reason for her going to this isolated spot.

It could be Mara wanted to remove her confining disguise and have a rendezvous with Quentin there. This thought impressed itself on Anita's mind, so much so that she determined to follow the mysterious woman and see what might be going on. She started down the hilly field and within a few minutes was close to the cemetery's iron fence.

In the meantime the veiled figure in black had vanished inside the cemetery and been lost in its maze of headstones, trees and tombs. Anita felt that she would regain sight of the veiled woman again as soon as she entered the cemetery. She felt she could keep in the background and use the gravestones to shield her from sight as she followed the woman's activities in the fenced area.

Entering by the rusty gate she realized that the cemetery was larger than she'd judged it from far off. It covered quite an area. The ground was uneven and the cemetery shaded by the adjacent forest. It was a dark and eerie place, even on a sunny day. She hesitated by a thin, slanted gravestone with its lettering worn away. There was no sign of the veiled woman. She stood very still and listened as she gazed at the awesome array of tombstones. Then she thought she saw the shadow of someone moving far ahead to the left.

Cautiously she went forward. She'd only gone a few paces when a mocking cry from above her made her halt. A chill of horror went through her. A shadow came low over her head and she saw that it had only been a crow coming out of the forest, crying out, and flying low over her to satisfy its curiosity.

With a small sigh of relief she rebuked herself for being so easily alarmed. And then as she stared straight ahead she saw the weird veiled figure studying a gravestone before moving on. She waited until the woman was out of sight again and followed her.

She disliked walking over the raised mounds marking the resting places of the Collinwood dead, so she tried to seek out a path between the graves and the headstones. The occasional tomb standing above ground gave her no problem. And there were several of these, along with two or three examples of graveyard statuary as tributes to the fact that some of the Collins family had boasted of imaginations.

An angel in gray marble with pious face and spreading wings guarded one grave, a figure of an ancient bearded prophet graced another while the most impressive of all was a carriage with empty seats completely chipped out of marble. She hesitated by this and strained her eyes to see some sign of the solitary black figure.

Not having any luck she moved on and mounted a small rise. Suddenly she was within a dozen feet of the veiled woman. The mysterious figure was standing before a Collins tomb and reading the inscription on it. Startled by having come upon her so soon, Anita quietly backed up until she was out of sight. At the same time she also lost her own view of the woman and the tomb.

She waited for a little until she was reasonably sure the woman had moved on. Then she mounted the rise once more and there was no sign of her. She went down by the tomb and saw it had a rusty iron door. And there was no lock on the door which appeared to be slightly ajar. At once she felt her heart begin to pound more rapidly as she realized that the veiled woman might have entered the tomb for some reason.

Anita stood there deliberating for a moment. She gazed around her, and seeing no sign of the eerie black figure anywhere, she decided to try the rusty iron door. Hesitantly she went down the several moss-covered steps and then reached out to grasp the latch and open the tomb door.

Just as she did so a voice from behind her asked, "Are you so anxious to enter the world of the dead, Miss Burgess?"

CHAPTER 9

Anita whirled around in terror to see Quentin Collins standing on the ground above her smirking. She had no idea how he had managed to get there without her hearing him or how long he had been following her.

She said, "Why did you scare me so?"

"I had no intention of alarming you," he said in his suave fashion.

She stood uncertainly by the door of the tomb. "I came down here and found this tomb interesting."

"Yes. I know you came down here," he said in his mocking fashion. "I've been behind you as you dodged between the gravestones. A most amazing performance if I may say so."

Anita swallowed hard. She saw that the best way out of her embarrassment was to tell him the truth. She said, "I was out for a walk and I saw your friend's widow come down here."

"Are you sure?"

"Yes. I recognized her black dress and veil."

"Odd," he said. "I'm just as certain she was at Collinwood when I left."

She at once realized he didn't want her to know about the veiled woman being down there. That was why he was denying it. His presence there also fitted into her conception of what had been going on. Quentin and Mara (if the woman was Mara as Jeffrey insisted) had planned a meeting in the cemetery and she had interrupted it. She still had a feeling that the veiled figure had gone inside the tomb.

She said, "I'm sure that woman came into the cemetery. I saw her several times. I had an idea she entered this tomb and that is why I was about to open the door when you came up behind me."

"So that was it," Quentin said. "In that case we should certainly investigate the tomb."

Either he was a superb bluffer or he knew very well that the veiled woman was not in the tomb. She couldn't guess which was the case. But now that he was there she wasn't much interested in finding out.

She said, "It doesn't matter."

"But it does!" he insisted and he came down the moss-covered steps to stand beside her and shove the rusty iron door of the tomb open to reveal a dark and dusty vault with coffins stacked on either side of it.

She backed away from the opening. "She's not in there," she said in a taut voice.

Quentin smiled at her in his overbearing fashion. "Surely you're not afraid of the grave?"

"I'm not particularly fond of tombs or coffins," she said.

"I'd hoped you'd go in and search the place with me," he challenged her.

"No!"

"Who knows? We might find ourselves a skeleton or at least a skull in good condition."

She gave him a scathing look. "If I remember, you have more interest in skulls than most people."

Quentin looked amused. "Yes, I remember, you did see my ritual room in Venice."

She turned and started up the steps to the ground level and he yanked the tomb door closed and followed her. She moved a short distance away to a spot under a tall tree with a wide branch spread. He came and stood facing her.

He said, "I think you should be convinced now that you made an error. My friend did not come down here."

She was going to argue the point but decided against it. Instead she said, "I'm glad I came. It's a most interesting place."

His eyes mocked her. "In spite of your fears of skulls and skeletons."

"I'm thinking of its picturesque qualities on the surface," she said. "I prefer not to dwell on what may be under the ground."

"Probably that's a healthy approach," he said. "I agree that it is a rather lovely if somewhat brooding spot. I suppose one day I shall join my ancestors here."

"You plan to remain at Collinwood then?"

"I do," he said. "It becomes more my home every day." He gave her an earnest look. "Would you consider making it your home as well?"

She pretended not to understand the implication of what he said. "I'm not sure I like Maine that much," she told him.

"Is it Maine or the people in it you object to?"

Again Anita fended off the question by telling him, "I doubt that I'm ready to settle down anywhere yet."

"That is a mistake," he warned her. "It is time you found yourself a husband and a home."

The breeze rustled through the branches of the tree above her making a lonely sound. She realized she was a long distance away from the main house at Collinwood. It gave her an uneasy feeling to be here in the isolated cemetery with this young man she distrusted so greatly.

She said, "I saw someone come down here."

"Perhaps it was a ghost."

"In daylight?"

He nodded. "There have been ghosts seen in this very cemetery at high noon."

She stared at Quentin incredulously. "Phantoms in the blazing sun? I've never heard of such a thing."

"You should learn more about the legends of Collinwood," Quentin said. "You'd find them fascinating. I was told of the ghost of which I speak when I was a small boy. I was always interested in the supernatural."

"And your interest continues?"

"In one way or another," he said with a smile. "The story is that years ago a wife of one of the young sea captains of the Collins line died in childbirth. It was the custom in those days for young wives to go to sea with their captain husbands. But she was of delicate health and with a baby expected the local doctor advised her to remain here where she could get proper treatment."

"And she died anyway?"

"Unfortunately," Quentin said. "It was a sad occasion, the double burial of mother and child. A good many friends and relatives gathered here for the graveside ceremony. And while the minister was reading the service several of those standing by the open grave were startled to observe the youthful form of her captain husband push his way through the mourners to stand by the coffins."

"He managed to get there in time for the service," she said, caught up by the drama of the story.

"He did," Quentin said. "And those that were aware of his unexpected presence remarked on the look of sadness on his countenance. He bowed his head and stood there silently under the hot sun as the coffins were lowered into the ground."

"How awful for him."

"It must have been," Quentin agreed. "And then before anyone could step up to sympathize with him he broke away from the group and vanished in the direction of this tree by which we stand."

She gave a tiny shudder. "You make it seem very real."

"It is a true story of Collinwood," Quentin assured her. "My grandparents were present when it happened. They at once tried to locate the young man and comfort him. But he couldn't be found anywhere in the graveyard. It caused a good deal of worry. The general impression was that the tragedy had unhinged him and he'd gone off to commit suicide."

"Had he?"

"The group broke and many of them went back to Collinwood for the usual heavy meal and drinks that it was customary to serve to the relatives and mourners who had come a long way. Still there was no sign of the young captain. And then amid the relaxed conversation that followed the feasting and drinking, there came a discussion of whether or not the young man had worn a jacket at the graveside."

"I can't see that it was important," she said.

"It seemed so to them. One was sure he had on his blue captain's jacket with its gold buttons. Another said he wore a plain black coat. And still another said he was wearing a shirt open at the neck with a string of vines hanging down from his shoulders. Since this fellow had taken a little too much to drink nobody paid any attention to him."

"No wonder," she said.

"But later, when the young captain still didn't appear, and this man had sobered up, he still clung to his version of what the young man had been wearing. When he told the story now he said it was either vines or seaweed he'd seen draped from the bereaved captain's shoulders."

"What happened to the captain?"

Quentin gave her a knowing look. "They didn't learn that until a month later. Then the word came in the mail from London. The captain's ship had been lost in a storm off Spain and he'd gone down with it. It happened only a few days before the death of his wife and baby. His body had been recovered and buried in a small coastal town. When they found it there was a string of seaweed draped around his shoulders!"

Anita gasped. "So he was the ghost who appeared here at noon!"

"Yes," Quentin said. "And I understand on the anniversary of that burial day, and I've forgotten what date it is, if the sun shines the young captain still appears and stands for a few minutes by the graves."

"You'll make me afraid to come here at any time," she said, shivering.

"Your good friend Barnabas prefers to come here under the cover of darkness," Quentin said in his taunting way. "I don't suppose you think of him as a ghoul-like creature who prefers the company of the dead to the living."

"I can't believe that he does," she said. "He's charming."

"I'm surprised," Quentin said. "You're usually so astute. And yet you don't seem to have seen through Barnabas as yet."

"I'd prefer not to speak of him if you can't discuss him in a friendly way," she told the young squire of Collinwood.

"Then by all means let us avoid discussing him at all," Quentin said. "I would prefer that he never showed himself at Collinwood."

"I suppose he thinks he has as much right here as you."

"The estate was left to me. He, like Jasper and Georgina, have only the privilege of staying here as guests. It is my property now!"

"I see," she said.

Quentin gave her a strange look. "While we're on the subject of ghosts there is something I should tell you. Collinwood has lately been visited by a new phantom."

"Another ghost to add to the many?"

His hypnotic eyes fixed on hers. "One with a special meaning to both of us."

Fear clutched at her heart as she gazed into those sinister eyes. "What do you mean?"

"Lately a new phantom has been seen in the building of Collinwood and also on the grounds. A spectral form in a glittering white flowing dress."

"And?"

"It is Mara," he said simply.

She frowned. "I don't believe it."

"You had better," he said. "For you will undoubtedly see her before you leave here."

"Mara died in Venice. Why should she appear here?"

"For the same reason that young sea captain who was drowned in Spain made his appearance in this very cemetery. She is unhappy. A lost soul in the spirit world, restless and unable to find peace. So she has followed me here."

Anita stared at him, wondering what motive he might have in telling her this. Why had he deliberately brought Mara into things? There had to be a reason.

She said, "It's too incredible."

"So is Mara's ghost," he said grimly. "You'll remember I warned you that Mara suffered from the Gorgon curse. That at times her lovely face became one of shocking ugliness? Well, it seems in her spirit form the ugly face is the one that is seen. She confronted me in the upper hallway late one night and the sight of her made me ill."

She said, "I'll believe it only when she appears before me."

"That could happen any time," he said. "I realized this and wanted to give you some warning."

It was another unsettling complication. She'd had enough of ghosts and graveyards and was anxious to walk back to the cottage. She told him this and they started walking out of the cemetery together. She had no idea why he had shown up there if not to meet the veiled woman whom she believed to be Mara. And then it struck her!

Of course he had told her this gruesome story about Mara's ghost to throw her completely off the track. If she were to guard herself against Mara dead she would surely not think of the lovely dark girl as alive! And that was what he wanted. By his announcement of the ghost he not only hoped to terrify her but also convince her that Mara was buried back in Venice and not alive at Collinwood with her face hidden by a black veil.

He was still as wily as ever. As they walked towards the open cemetery gates she said, "Do you have a room at Collinwood the same as you had in your palace in Venice? One with a skull and black drapes?"

Quentin gave her a smiling glance. "You're asking me if I'm still dabbling in black magic?"

"Yes. I know you usually deny it. But surely you can be frank with me."

"I have always continued certain of my investigations of the supernatural," he said.

"And are the girls here, Georgina, Laura Cranston and your widow friend, helping you with your rituals as the young women in Venice did?"

"They have been kind enough to allow me to call on them," he admitted. "They are not like you. You have never been friendly to my experiments."

"We can't all have the same tastes," she said bitterly.

"I allow for that," he agreed. "I still think you could be the most sensitive and helpful of any of them."

"Don't count on me."

"I never give up hope," he said. "I think when you have fully recovered from your grief at Arnold's tragic death, you will throw your lot in with me."

"I wonder," she said. She had to leave it open to help progress her brother's scheme of revenge.

They were emerging from the cemetery into the field when they were suddenly confronted by an irate Laura Cranston. The pretty dark girl's eyes were flashing with anger. She wore a riding costume with a dainty flat-topped hat pinned jauntily in her upsweep of hair. And in her hand was a riding crop which Anita thought she might be ready to use on her.

"So this is where you've been while I've waited for you?" Laura said angrily.

Quentin seemed embarrassed. "I was showing Anita the cemetery."

"So I see," Laura said with sarcasm. "And you both apparently found it so interesting you forgot that I was to meet you out here."

"I hadn't forgotten," he said, placatingly. "I had an idea I was too early."

"You couldn't have," Laura snapped. "We carefully set the time."

Anita turned to the young man. "I'll go on by myself. I know you have things to say to Miss Cranston."

"How generous of you!" Laura Cranston purred with biting sarcasm.

Quentin looked pale and uneasy. "Perhaps you had better do that," he said. "I'll see you later at Collinwood or the cottage."

"Yes, Miss Burgess," the angry dark girl said. "You needn't worry. I'm sure Quentin means to continue paying you court."

"You've taken the wrong meaning out of this," Anita told her quietly. "I'm sorry." And she hurriedly left them.

She walked straight up the field to the old house without looking back. She imagined Laura Cranston had ridden as far as the cemetery and tied her horse somewhere while she waited for Quentin. The suave young man had undoubtedly kept her waiting a long while but Anita had no doubts that he'd manage to soothe her ruffled feelings.

Passing the old house, she looked for some sign of life again but the place still had that deserted appearance. So she went on towards Collinwood. There she paused to enjoy the gardens to the left of the mansion and while strolling along one of the gravel walks encountered the attractive Georgina. Jasper Collins's daughter had a wicker basket on her arm filled with cut flowers and she carried a pair of shears.

She seemed surprised to see Anita. "I had no idea you were in the garden," the blonde girl said.

"I suppose I am a trespasser," Anita smiled. "But the flowers looked so lovely I stopped to admire them."

"You're very welcome," Georgina said.

"The garden must take a lot of work."

"It does. But we have a good man," Georgina said. "I understand your brother is in the village today. The stable man provided him with a horse and carriage."

"He had a few things he wanted to do," Anita said. "So I took a stroll as far as the old cemetery. I met Quentin and Laura Cranston down there."

Georgina's eyebrows lifted a shade. "Oh, so that is where they both are," she said, a note of coldness in her voice.

Anita at once was aware there was some rivalry among Quentin's present collection of beauties. She had not made the statement deliberately but it had at least offered this new perspective of things at Collinwood.

She said, "I was sure I saw the widow friend of Quentin's down there as well."

The blonde girl shook her head. "You're wrong in that. Evelyn has been sitting in the garden all afternoon." She pointed. "See, she's over by that hedge, seated on a bench."

Anita glanced in the direction Georgina had indicated and saw the veiled woman was sitting there. She appeared to be in a state of deep thought. She had no book to read or anything to distract her.

Anita said, "I would think she'd be warm in the hot sun with that veil and dark dress. At least she could remove the veil."

"She'd never do that," Georgina assured her.

"Not even if you suggested it?"

"Quentin has asked us not to interfere with her, so naturally we don't." There was a firm note in the blonde's voice.

"It's too bad," she said. "She seems so unhappy."

"The only one she'll talk to is Quentin," the other girl said. "And only when they are alone."

"I hope she improves."

"I'm sure she will," Georgina said. "Would you like to take some roses back to the cottage with you?"

"I don't want to deprive you," she protested.

Georgina said, "You won't. We have plenty."

As the blonde girl gathered some of the flowers in a cone of newspaper for her, Anita found the courage to ask, "You have a servant Quentin brought back from Italy, haven't you?"

The blonde girl eyed her cagily. "You mean Mirabelle."

"Yes. I think that is her name."

"She's very efficient now that she has learned some of our ways," the girl said. "In the beginning she had difficulties with several of the local maids. You know the resentment small town folk have against foreigners."

"I have an idea."

"Mirabelle was libeled by one of the girls. She spread stories all around the village about her. But I think the sensation is over with now. And we have a smooth working staff."

"Quentin must have felt she was competent or he wouldn't have brought her all the long journey here," she said. She thought this might stimulate some reaction.

Georgina looked slightly unhappy. "I dare say he could have done just as well here. But since he brought her I felt we should try to adapt to her."

"Of course."

"You met Quentin in Venice. You said so last night."

"My brother and I were there when he had the Castle Asariana."

"I hear it was a kind of palace."

"Very elaborate."

"More so than Collinwood?"

Anita smiled. "It is hardly possible to compare the two places. Both are outstanding in their own way."

"I suppose so," Georgina said, a note of doubt in her voice. "I hope you enjoy the flowers." And she handed them to her.

She took them. "I will."

"You said you saw Quentin and Laura down by the cemetery?"

"They were there when I left."

Georgina showed uneasiness. "I wonder what is keeping them so long."

"I think Laura was riding. She may have gone on somewhere and Quentin could have returned to the outbuildings and the workmen."

"I suppose so," the other girl said vaguely. "I must go see if he is there."

They parted and Anita walked back along the cliffs to the cottage. She could tell there was a strong rivalry and jealousy between the blonde Georgina and the dark Laura for Quentin's affections. Something like this could cause a real rift in his group. And Mirabelle fitted in somewhere. She was no servant, at least she hadn't been, back in Italy. She had been a member of his coven of witches. And this brought up Mara. Was she there in the disguise of veil and black gown?

These thoughts filled her mind as she approached the cottage. When she reached it and took out her key to unlock the door, she was surprised to hear footsteps coming from around the side of the house and a moment later the elderly Jasper Collins came into sight. The old man limped up to her with a smile on his lined face.

"I've been sitting out back waiting for you to come home," he said.

She couldn't imagine why he had come but felt it would be wise to be pleasant to him. She said, "I've been for a walk and Georgina gave me these flowers."

"She's got a green thumb, that girl," the old man said with satisfaction. "She used to give instructions to all the gardeners. Now she hardly goes into the garden. Not since that Quentin arrived!"

Anita smiled. "Well, she was there today. My brother went to the village but he should be back soon. Won't you come in?"

"Don't mind if I do," the old man said. He limped in after her and found himself a worn leather upholstered chair and sank into it so heavily that its springs protested.

She busied herself getting a vase for the flowers and putting some water in it. As she worked, she said, "I went as far as the cemetery."

Jasper Collins gave a mirthless chuckle. "That's as far as most of us will go."

"It's an interesting old place," she said. "But scary!"

Jasper's expression became grim. "There ain't any part of Collinwood isn't scary today. That Quentin has brought a cloud over the estate."

She placed the vase of flowers on the living room table and then stood back to study them. "Have things here changed so?"

"Gets worse every day," Jasper Collins complained. "When a man's own daughter turns against him for someone like Quentin!"

"You feel that Georgina is fascinated by him?"

"She does everything he asks," the old man said. "When they hold those black magic meetings upstairs she's the first to go."

"Quentin does hold the gatherings frequently?"

"Almost every night. And that Mirabelle is one of the ringleaders. There's more to her than she lets on."

"I'm sure of it," Anita agreed. Then she asked the old man the question that had been bothering her. "What about the widow in the veil? Does she take part?"

"She must," Jasper Collins said. "She goes up there. I know that. But then you never hear her say anything. According to Quentin she's some crazy, but then you don't know whether he's lying or not."

"Have you ever seen her face?"

"No. She never takes off that veil."

"I think that's very strange," Anita said.

"And even stranger that she don't say a word. Just nods and makes signs. It gets on my nerves."

"I'm sure it must," she said.

"But there are other and worse things going on," the old man said unhappily. "I told you I saw the werewolf?"

"You did."

"And that's been since Quentin come. I say he's the one to blame. He either is the creature himself or someone along with him is doing it. A lot of people have left Collinsport because of the werewolf scare."

"My brother saw some strange tracks in the sand. And he claims they were too large to belong to a dog."

"I don't doubt it. The werewolf roams around down there under the moonlight. But the most scary of all is the new ghost."

She held her breath. "The new ghost?"

"The one that has followed that Quentin from Italy. All in white and with a face so ugly it sends a chill down your spine. That's the one you best watch out for!"

Anita listened with a sinking sensation. She thought Quentin had made up the story of Mara's ghost simply to frighten her. But here was proof that someone else had actually seen itl

CHAPTER 10

Old Jasper Collins stayed at the cottage only a short time. After he left Anita began preparing the evening meal for her brother and herself. She hoped by keeping occupied she wouldn't be so nervous. But she still found herself on edge. So many shocking things had come her way since the morning. And perhaps this story of Mara's ghost haunting the estate was the most worrisome. She counted on Barnabas arriving early in the evening and felt he might be able to offer some explanations. He usually had a good idea of the meaning behind the rumors and gossip. And she would be able to discuss it all with Jeffrey.

There was also David Benson. She had only known the young man for a short time but he had made an excellent impression on her. He was surely on her side even if he wasn't as expert in the supernatural as someone like Barnabas Collins. Unless the situation changed she would need all their help.

Quentin was growing more brazen in his admissions. He had not tried to deny to her that he'd already set up a black magic circle at Collinwood. In fact he'd even tried to enlist her in it as he had once before in Venice. He seemed sure that eventually she would weaken and join him in this Satanist worship.

The other young women he'd gathered around him were too hypnotized by his charm to question what he was doing. Just as those unfortunate girls at the palace in Venice had dedicated their lives to him so it was with Georgina and the rest. But there was one difference of which she was aware. There was jealousy between his supporters here. If she could find some way to use that, it could be of value in breaking up the cult and destroying Quentin's power.

Her brother returned a little before six. He entered the cottage with a somewhat discouraged expression. She did not question him about his day at once but waited until he had relaxed a little and they were seated at the table.

Then she asked him, "How did it go with you in the village?"

He sighed. "A strange, bewildering day."

"Why do you say that?"

"You encounter so many opinions. It seemed that almost everyone I met had some different idea of what is going on out here."

"Collinwood is a popular subject of conversation then?"

"I would gather that it always has been," her brother said bitterly. "And then I think some of the people I talked with might have been less than frank with me."

"Why should they distrust you?"

"I'm an outsider. In small, isolated communities like Collinsport any one from the outside is regarded with suspicion."

She nodded. "I can see that."

"So I first had to break down that barrier. And once I thought I had I asked the most pertinent questions I could think of."

"Did you discover anything new?"

"Yes and no."

Anita gave him a thin smile. "You're almost as hard to interpret as the people you were questioning."

"I suppose after a day like this I've picked up some of their manner," he admitted. "The fact is they do feel something evil is going on here. And that Quentin is responsible."

"That is not new to us."

"No. But I wanted to hear it from them. Most of them resent that Quentin was left the estate. They thought the Jasper Collins branch was going to get it. In spite of his bad temper, the old man seems to be popular."

"I like him," she agreed. "He seems very honest. He came by here for a short time this afternoon."

Jeffrey showed interest. "I'm sorry I missed him."

"He said he'd be back again. What else did you hear in the village?"

"This werewolf scare is very real."

"And they link it with Quentin?"

"Yes. There have been two killings in the area and a number

of people claim to have seen the strange creature stalking the countryside at night."

"They link Quentin with its appearance because it has only shown itself since his return?"

"That's about it. And that maid he discharged claims she was in the room he uses as a black magic headquarters. Her talk has done him the most harm."

"I would guess she's telling the truth."

"I don't question any of it. From her description it's the same sort of place Quentin showed you in that palace in Venice. I'd say if there is another of these werewolf killings the local people will take the law into their own hands and come out here and raid Collinwood."

She opened her eyes wide. "The feeling is running that high?"

"It is. They are sick of these macabre happenings at Collinwood. It seems from the start the Collins family has been tainted by one curse after another. It began long ago with the first Barnabas Collins being dubbed a vampire and the stories of phantoms roaming the estate have spread over the years until we now come to the case of Quentin being accused of transforming himself into a werewolf."

She gave her brother a questioning look. "What did you hear about the present Barnabas Collins?"

Jeffrey sighed. "There's so much talk about black magic and the werewolf that no one seems interested in Barnabas Collins at the moment. I couldn't get any interest in him. I'd start to ask questions about Barnabas and they'd say he was a strange one. Then they'd at once add that Quentin was even stranger and more evil. After that I couldn't get them off the subject of the werewolf."

In a way she found herself pleased by this news. At least Barnabas wasn't resented by the people in Collinsport in the same way that Quentin was. They might think him eccentric and aloof but for the moment at least there was no real hatred of him. This discounted some of the slanderous things Quentin had said about him.

She said, "It seems to all add up to a general suspicion and dislike of Quentin."

"The villagers are quite upset about him," Jeffrey agreed.

"I may have gotten more information right here than you managed in the village," she said with a wan smile. And she told him of her walk to the cemetery and what had gone on there.

Jeffrey listened with avid interest. "If there is enough jealousy between those girls we may eventually get one of them to testify against Quentin," he said.

"I thought of that," she agreed. "I think the most tension

exists between Georgina and Laura Cranston. They are undoubtedly rivals."

"And both high-spirited!"

"But there is also Mirabelle and the widow in the black veil."

"Unknown quantities," he agreed. "Though I'm almost certain the woman hiding her face is Mara. I'm positive her suicide was staged."

"I don't know," she said. "What about this ghost story? That Mara is the latest phantom to haunt Collinwood?"

Jeffrey got up from the table and began to pace again. "It could be a story put out by Quentin to stop us from thinking Mara is alive."

"I thought of that."

Her brother continued to pace. "It's the most likely explanation."

"And the reason the veiled woman hid herself from me in the cemetery was that it was Mara. And she was afraid of me penetrating her disguise."

"Very likely."

"And Quentin distracted my attention while she got away and went back to the gardens at Collinwood. Georgina thought she had never left there but she needn't have noticed if she was only absent a short time."

Jeffrey came to a halt in front of her. "It all fits perfectly. Including Quentin's being in the cemetery. He and Mara had planned a meeting and you spoiled it."

She reminded him, "But Laura was waiting for him outside the cemetery. He had promised to meet her there."

"After he talked with Mara no doubt," Jeffrey said. "You know how wily he is."

"I know too well," she said sadly. "But there is one other thing to consider."

"What?"

"Jasper Collins said he saw this ghost. His description of it was identical to the one I'd heard before. And he is an honest old man. He must have seen something."

"Quentin could have arranged that. He might have gotten Mara to do it herself."

"I suppose so. He went over that business of the ugly face and Mara's being under the Gorgon curse when he talked of the ghost today. The face that strikes men dead."

"I'm familiar with the Medusa legend," Jeffrey said. "And I think Quentin is using it for his own purposes."

She gave a small sigh. "Just the same it frightens me."

Jeffrey looked grim. "I confess I'm more afraid of Mara living than Mara dead."

"And there is something very sinister about that creature in the black dress and veil. Just looking at her sets my nerves on edge."

"She emanates evil," Jeffrey said. "That is why I'm sure that it is Mara in disguise."

"How can we find out?"

"We'll have to wait for our opportunity," Jeffrey said.

"Perhaps Barnabas can help us," she suggested. "He told me he'd try to call here at the cottage tonight."

"I'd like to meet him," her brother said.

"Did you see David Benson in the village today?"

"No. He didn't seem to be around. And I didn't go to his home. I had too many other things to do."

"He is very nice," she said. "And I know he's interested in our welfare."

Jeffrey gave her a thin smile. "Your welfare would be closer to it. But he does seem to be a very responsible person."

After dinner she began to worry about Barnabas and when he might arrive. The warm day had ended in a cool evening and as a result fog was moving in from the bay. This caused it to become dark earlier. By eight o'clock the fog shrouded the grounds of Collinwood and the foghorn at the point was giving out its mournful warning at regular intervals.

She had gone to her bedroom for a little and now she stared out the window into the foggy darkness and tried to guess what might be keeping Barnabas. While she knew his promise to visit them had been somewhat vague she had felt he would come. But the evening was going by and so far there had been no sign of him.

Jeffrey was out in the living room reading, waiting for Barnabas's possible arrival. Her tension began to shift to pure annoyance. It seemed he was going to fail her, and she hadn't thought of him as that sort of person. Then she began to wonder if he were merely shy. Hesitating to visit the cottage because of her brother being there. He did not meet people with any ease.

She worried about this until she made up her mind to put on her cloak and go out in search of him. He might be lurking outside only a short distance away. She had no intention of wandering far from the house but she felt it would be wise to at least take a look in the immediate area.

Going out to the living room, she said, "I'm taking a short walk. I need some fresh air."

Jeffrey at once put aside his newspaper and got up. "I'll go with you," he said.

"I'd rather you wouldn't."

"But it may be dangerous for you out there," he protested.

"I won't go so far that I can't call to you if I'm frightened," she said.

"That's taking a lot for granted," he warned her. "You could be attacked in a manner that wouldn't allow you to cry out."

She knew this was so. But balanced against her urgent desire to find Barnabas it didn't matter. "The truth is I think Barnabas might be waiting out there somewhere to see me."

"He must see the lights of the cottage. Why doesn't he come here?"

"He's very retiring," she said. "He might want to avoid a meeting with you."

Jeffrey looked puzzled. "Why should he want to avoid me?"

"He's that way with people," she said. "I promise not to go far."

And before Jeffrey protested further she hurried out the cottage door into the damp, thick fog. She'd had no idea how heavy it was from inside. Now glancing in the direction of Collinwood, only a relatively short distance away, she could barely see the glow of its lights. And then only as formless yellow blobs against the grayish darkness.

She tightened her cloak around her and stood staring for a moment, looking for a sign of someone. But there seemed to be no one out on this wretched night. Glancing back at the cottage, she was reassured by the lights from it. And gathering her courage she ventured a short distance further in the direction of the cliffs.

Barnabas, she had heard, often walked there. She thought it possible he might be strolling there now. The warning of the foghorn was mixed with the lash of the waves on the beach to create an eerie atmosphere. Every bush, branch and tree took on a ghostly, menacing air in the fog. No wonder the isolated estate had won a reputation for harboring phantoms!

Without realizing it, she had gone further from the cottage than she intended and still no sign of Barnabas. She began to feel slight anger again. She had depended on him so! She continued on until she was actually at the brink of the cliff. Standing there feeling forlorn and deserted, she began to think of David Benson's young, pleasant face and wish that he would visit them again.

She was standing there thinking this when she finally saw a dark figure moving in the fog a distance away. A thrill of hope rushed through her and she called out, "Barnabas, is that you?"

There was no immediate reply. But she caught the outline of the shadowy figure again through a rift in the fog. She managed to get a glimpse of the caped coat that Barnabas habitually wore. With this to encourage her she rushed forward.

"Barnabas!" she called out again.

She almost slipped and stumbled on the wet path, then carefully regaining her balance she went on until she was within a half-dozen feet of the mysterious figure. She could see now that its back was turned to her. The only thing she could make out clearly was a long black cloak and a hood. This was not Barnabas.

A warning shock cut through her like pain. She halted and stared at this odd stranger who shared the murky night with her. Then in a swift movement the figure whirled around with the cloak thrown back to reveal a girl in a filmy white dress with a flowing skirt. But what terrified and sickened her was the unbelievable ugliness of the girl's face. It was too horrible to note clearly with one eye lower than the other, the nose twisted, the mouth sagging and ending in a monstrously disfigured chin. It was like something a mad artist might have drawn!

And now the creature stretched out its hands and came slowly towards her. Anita gazed at the advancing horror and screamed and promptly blacked out!

"Answer me!" The voice came faintly through to her. She opened her eyes and looked up into Jeffrey's alarmed face.

"At least you're alive!" he said.

Terror raced back into her mind. She raised herself up from the wet grass where she'd fallen and stared into the fog frantically. "Where did she go?"

"Who?"

"The ghost!" she said, turning eyes wide with fear to him. "I saw Mara's ghost! And that gruesome-looking face! Everything they said about the Gorgon curse is true!"

"I found you alone," he said. "I heard you call out and came as fast as I could."

"I screamed out when I saw her awful face!" she said, still suffering from the shock of it.

"Are you able to get up?"

"Yes," she said, and allowed him to help her to her feet.

"We'll gain nothing but a possible cold by remaining out here," he told her. "Let's go back to the cottage and you can tell me what happened."

"All right," she said. Her teeth were chattering and she was trembling as a result of the fright and exposure. She was content to have him offer his arm around her for comfort and support as they made their way through the fog back to the cottage.

Once there he gave her a hot drink and then sat down opposite her to question her. "You say you saw Mara's ghost?"

She sipped the hot drink and nodded. "Yes. The Gorgon face!

It had to be her! That face was more horrible than you can imagine. If she changed in that way the night Arnold was with her it explains his accident. The mere shock of seeing her that way could have made him stumble on the stairs."

"Possibly," her brother said in his careful way.

"I'd heard that she sometimes was transformed into nightmarish ugliness but I had to see it to believe it."

"Perhaps that is what Quentin decided," her brother said.

She frowned over the mug of hot liquid. "What do you mean?"

"He could have staged this ghostly appearance for your benefit. To convince you of the Gorgon curse story and also that Mara was truly dead."

She sighed and considered this. "You could be right. But I don't know. She came towards me."

"Yet when I discovered you there was no one near. You were on the ground alone."

She shuddered. "I don't know what to think."

Jeffrey had lit his pipe and now he puffed on it thoughtfully. "Which is probably exactly what Quentin wants."

She looked at her brother anxiously. "I think we should leave."

He frowned. "Now, when we may be close to settling with Quentin?"

"I don't think we are. He's playing with us like puppets. He mocks us and goes on with his evil."

"You're too upset to make a sound decision about this now," he warned her.

"I've been against this from the first," she said, near tears. "I didn't want to come here. I was sure nothing good would result from it. But you insisted. Now that we're here things are even worse than we guessed. Quentin is so strong in his evil we can't fight him."

"I don't think you really believe that," Jeffrey said, his eyes meeting hers in a troubled gaze.

She looked down to avoid his eyes. "It's like opposing Satan!"

"A worthy adversary," Jeffrey said. "Some of the finest people have devoted a lifetime to just that."

"It will end with one or the other of us being killed just as Arnold was," she said. "Probably both of us."

"I'm willing to take that risk," her brother said. "And I hoped that you were."

"I don't know any longer," she said.

Their discussion was interrupted by a gentle knocking on the door of the cottage. Then it was opened and Barnabas Collins came in to join them. His appearance made Anita feel better almost at once. She got to her feet and rushed to him.

"I thought you weren't coming," she said.

He smiled at her. "I didn't promise I would be early."

"It's true, you didn't," she admitted. "You haven't met my brother." And she introduced him to Jeffrey.

The two men shook hands and she could tell they would get on well. Barnabas moved on into the room and stood before the fireplace looking regal and stern. His eyes showed concern and his thin lips compressed as he heard about her meeting with the phantom.

"It was a mistake for you to venture out there on your own," was the first opinion Barnabas offered.

Jeffrey spoke up. "I told her the same thing."

Barnabas eyed her gravely. "You should listen to your brother's advice."

She shrugged. "I went out there looking for you."

"That was stupid," Barnabas said without making his reproach sound too unpleasant. "You put yourself in needless danger."

"At least I did see Mara's ghost," she said.

"What you thought was Mara's ghost," Jeffrey corrected her.

"It was too horrible to be other than the real thing," she said.

Barnabas said, "I'd like you to describe what you saw again."

She did, faltering at the description of that nightmare face and ending with, "I didn't believe in the Gorgon curse until I saw that face."

Barnabas showed no reaction to her words. "I agree with your brother," he said. "You can't be sure that Mara is dead. She could be the veiled woman. And in that case the ghost you saw was some contrived performance."

Anita stared at him in surprise. "I was sure I could count on your believing me. You know so much of what is going on here."

Barnabas looked at them grimly. "I'm almost as puzzled as both of you. When I encountered Quentin in Venice I was repulsed by what he was doing there. I could not remain in a house where such evil practices were taking place. I had no idea he would flee to America and begin over again."

"Which is what he has done," Jeffrey said.

"Exactly," Barnabas said, frowning. "You know that he bears the werewolf curse?"

"We have heard it," she said.

"He does. I think that is what made him enter his compact with the Devil. He feels if he pays enough tribute through introducing others to his evil cult he will win freedom for himself."

Jeffrey frowned. "Does he have any control over this

werewolf thing? Does he transform his body only at his own desire?"

"I think that may have been so in the beginning," Barnabas said. "But not any longer. The spells come on him and he cannot help himself. This has driven him into madness."

"As revealed in his desire to enslave young women in his cult," she said.

"That is it," Barnabas said. "He has made helpless puppets of them all. I'm sure that hypnotism is involved. And maybe drugs. But Georgina, Laura Cranston and the others are as helplessly tied to him as were those pitiful girls in Venice."

She nodded. "He's tried to get me to join him. He still seems to think he will."

Barnabas gave her a warning glance. "If you're not more cautious it could be that he might involve you yet. He is crafty and will wait until the right moment."

Jeffrey sighed. "My sister feels we should leave. She claims I have placed both of us in needless danger. That Quentin is not our problem. He is too strong for us to fight him."

Barnabas showed mild interest and then turned to her. "You didn't talk that way last night? You seemed determined to settle accounts with him."

"That was before I saw Mara's ghost," she admitted.

Barnabas studied her with those piercing brown eyes. "I think you are placing too much emphasis on that ghost."

"Perhaps," she said.

"It could have been any one of those girls wearing a mask to frighten you. Quentin probably put them up to it."

She sighed in vivid remembrance of the horror. "It didn't look like a mask."

"Still that is what it probably was," Barnabas said. "It is possible whoever it is may still be outside somewhere waiting for another opportunity to terrify you. To press that ugly mask against your window perhaps, or wait until someone else ventures into the night to see the grotesque face and spread the word. An impressionable maid from Collinwood or even a stableman."

"I agree," Anita's brother said. And to Barnabas, he added, "Why don't we go out and see if we can encounter this phantom and unmask her?"

"A good idea," Barnabas said.

Anita hesitated. "I don't know. And anyway I don't want to be left here alone."

Jeffrey said, "You'll be much safer in here than out in the fog and darkness."

"Just as long as you keep the cottage locked," Barnabas warned her.

And so they left her to go in search of Mara's ghost. She locked the door after them and watched from the window until they disappeared in the fog. Then a terrible premonition of danger took hold of her. She moved over to the fireplace and sat hunched in a chair before the dying embers. She was in a kind of panic. All she could think of was what they might be doing and how soon they would return.

Time dragged by and her tensions grew. She was about to put another log on the fire when the knock came on the door. She dropped the log and stood staring in the direction of the door with a terrified expression on her face. It couldn't be Barnabas and Jeffrey. They would identify themselves.

Then she thought of David Benson, and some of her fear abated. It had to be David. She'd been hoping he might pay her another visit. She went cautiously over to the door and listened. There was no sound from outside. Then the knock was repeated.

"Is it you, David?" she called out.

The muffled reply she received sounded like yes. So she at once drew back the heavy bolt and opened the door. Then she stumbled back as she saw the monstrous greenish-gray wolf crouched there snarling!

CHAPTER 11

The mad animal's amber eyes burned into her. With an anguished cry she turned and fled to the hallway and the haven of her bedroom beyond it. She heard the snarling creature behind her and could almost feel its hot breath. Yet she somehow managed to reach the bedroom and slam the door closed. Seconds later it sprang against the door but she had latched it and now stood with her weight pressed against it.

The door trembled under the assault and she feared it would only be a short while before the angry animal burst into the bedroom and attacked her. It had to be the werewolf of which so much had been rumored. Now she was experiencing its threat at firsthand. The thing sprang at the door again and it seemed the latch would give. She could hear the angry panting and snarling on the other side of the fairly thin wood.

She fixed her terrified eyes on the window and speculated on trying to escape that way. But she knew that once she was outside it would be simple for the animal to catch up with her. She would have no defense at all. Perhaps it would be better to wait and hope she could somehow hold it off.

There was a brief silence from outside and she waited for the next assault. But minutes passed and it did not come. Then she thought she heard the sound of voices. A moment later she recognized them as belonging to Barnabas and her brother. The two had come back. Her heart gave a great leap of relief. Yet she still did not make any move to unlock the door, unsure whether the mad creature was still out there or not.

Then she heard her brother speaking from the living room. There were footsteps coming towards the door of her room and someone rattled the handle of the bedroom door.

"Anita, where are you?" It was Jeffrey calling out to her.

"Here," she said. And she unlocked the door and met him in the hall.

"We found the front door of the cottage open," he exclaimed.

"I know," she said weakly.

He grasped her arm. "What was it?"

"The werewolf," she said, staring at him unhappily. "It got into the living room. I managed to escape in here."

Jeffrey led her out to the living room where Barnabas was waiting. "Did you hear that? The werewolf came here after her while we were out."

Barnabas shook his head. "Quentin must indeed be in a state of desperation. So the monster showed itself here."

"Yes," she said. "There was a knock on the door. I thought it was the young lawyer we'd met from Collinsport. I opened the door and the thing came after me!"

Jeffrey said bitterly, "While we were out chasing phantoms and found none!"

"The werewolf must have heard you coming and taken fright," Anita said. "I expected it to assault my bedroom door again but it didn't."

"Quentin wouldn't want us to find him here," Barnabas said.

She frowned in disbelief. "You think it was he who threatened me just now? That snarling, mad animal was Quentin?"

Barnabas's handsome face showed grim resignation. "If we are to believe the stories it had to be," he said. "There was no such animal roving the area before he returned."

Jeffrey said angrily, "He has to be destroyed in one form or the other."

Barnabas nodded. "Perhaps he'll venture into the village again tonight and this time he'll be shot down."

"Can a bullet cause his death?" Jeffrey wanted to know. "He is a supernatural creature!"

"If it strikes a vital area it would kill him," Barnabas said. "I believe he has been shot at several times but the bullets merely grazed him."

"What do we do now?" Jeffrey asked.

"I have a rather audacious idea," Barnabas said with a smile on his sallow handsome face. "I think your sister and I should pay a social call. A social call on Quentin at Collinwood."

Jeffrey frowned. "You must be joking!"

"I'm completely serious," Barnabas said. "How do you feel about it, Anita? Would you be willing to go with me while your brother waits here to see if any of the phantoms decide to return to the cottage?"

She gave him a wan smile. "I'll do whatever you think is best. But I must confess I don't understand the reasoning behind it."

"I first want to find out if Quentin is at Collinwood. Then I'd also like to see how he receives us. Whether his nerves are at all shaken up. And we'd have an additional opportunity to see what is going on there."

"Quentin won't welcome you," Jeffrey predicted. "He'll be angry at his failure here and he'll know why you've come to visit."

"Let him know!" Barnabas said disdainfully. "If we annoy him, so much the better."

"I'll go along with you," she said.

Jeffrey frowned at Barnabas. "You will be answerable to me for her safety, Collins."

"You needn't worry," Barnabas assured him. "She is safe as long as I'm with her."

"But suppose Quentin finds some way to separate you," Jeffrey worried. "Shouldn't I go as well? As an extra precaution?"

"I have an idea there could be a visitation from the ghost while we're at Collinwood," Barnabas told him. "That is why I'd prefer you'd remain."

"Very well," Jeffrey said, sounding less than satisfied. Barnabas helped her on with her cloak. And once again she was impressed by his gentlemanly ways. He was attentive and understanding as they left the cottage and started out into the fog-shrouded night. The lights of Collinwood showed faintly as they strolled across the lawn towards the great mansion.

He said, "I think you're a very brave girl."

"Not really," she told him. "I've been begging Jeffrey to leave here. I'm beginning to believe Quentin is more than a match for us."

"He is a dangerous opponent."

"You are better qualified to deal with him," she said. "You know him and his weaknesses."

"I am not without a certain weakness on my own part," he said.

She eyed his tall, broad-shouldered figure with disbelief. "I can't picture you as weak."

"Like many others in the Collins family I have had a serious problem," he said. "It is only that Quentin's evil doings outshine everything else that more attention is not coming my way. The people in Collinsport mistrust me."

"Why?"

He gave her a knowing glance. "I'm sure you must have heard some of the rumors about me."

"I've heard that you might be tainted with the vampire curse like your ancestor," she said. "Quentin was the one who made a great deal of it. But I knew he was lying."

"Even he occasionally tells the truth," Barnabas said in a quiet tone.

She glanced at him as he walked with her in the heavy fog, his profile showing a sad expression. "You can't mean there is anything in what he said?"

Once again Barnabas evaded answering her directly by saying, "No matter what, you can count on me as your friend."

"I know that," she said.

"But you have another friend," Barnabas said. "I mean this David Benson. The young man you thought was at the door when you opened it to the werewolf."

"I do like David."

"Is there a romance between you two?"

"I haven't known him long enough for that," she protested.

"Romance can bloom quickly," Barnabas told her. "And I think it is time you found yourself some young man who wants to marry you."

"It is also important that I want to marry him, isn't it?"

He smiled at her. "Don't you?"

"I'm not sure," she said. "Not at all sure. And I'd want to be before I made any decisions." She would have liked to have been completely honest and tell him that she was more than a little in love with him but it seemed neither the time nor the place.

They were close to the entrance of Collinwood and Barnabas halted and warned her. "I want you to leave everything to me."

"Of course," she said.

"If Quentin isn't at home we'll only stay for a few minutes," he went on to say. "I mostly want to observe him." They moved on to the steps of the stately house and Barnabas rang the bell.

They waited in the chill wet fog for some time before the door was opened. And then it was the ancient Jasper Collins who peered out at them. "Yes?" the old man said.

"It's Barnabas and Miss Burgess," Barnabas said. "We have come to call on Quentin."

The old man snorted with disgust. "You could have saved your time. He won't see you. He's upstairs conducting one of those rituals."

Barnabas at once was interested. "Surely we can come in for a while and wait."

"You can if you like," Jasper Collins said, holding the door open for them. "You can talk to me. Not that anybody seems to want to any more."

Barnabas gave her a knowing glance and then guided her inside. They went into the living room, the elderly Jasper limping ahead of them as he leaned firmly on his cane. They reached the fireplace area and Jasper let himself into an easy chair with a tiny moan. Barnabas showed her to a chair opposite the old man and stood facing them.

Barnabas asked Jasper Collins, "Was Quentin out tonight?"

The old man nodded. "Yes. He came back not much more than ten minutes ago. Seemed pale and queer. But he gets those spells often." He paused and peered up at Barnabas. "You know what they say about him. Well, when he got back tonight nothin' would do but he get all those females together and hold one of his black masses."

"Where does he hold them?" Barnabas asked.

"Third floor," Jasper said. "The first room on the right. I've never been in it since he fixed it up. But I guess from what that maid spread around it's a mighty strange place."

"I'd like to take a look at it," Barnabas said.

Jasper frowned. "It pays to keep a distance from the Devil and his works."

"How do you feel about that?" Barnabas asked her.

Her eyes met his. "I'm in agreement with you. It would be exciting to see it."

"Then why don't we go up?" he said.

Jasper pointed a skinny finger at them. "Don't tell him I let you know where it is or he'd make me suffer for it."

"You needn't worry about that," Barnabas promised him. Then he signaled to Anita to join him. "Let us quietly go up there."

Her heart beat more rapidly as they ascended the shadowed stairs in silence. She'd heard so much about these secret rituals that she was excited at the prospect of learning something about them. She was also nervous as to what Quentin's reaction would be. He could very well be angry at their intrusion, especially as he knew Barnabas was opposed to all this dabbling in black magic.

When they neared the third floor they could hear eerie organ music. It had a strange unearthly air and was not loud. When they came to the third landing, it was in darkness. Barnabas reached out and took her hand in his chill one and guided her down the hallway. They came to the room from which the organ music could be heard. There was a slit of light showing from under the door.

Barnabas whispered, "We'll try opening the door slowly. It may not be locked."

It wasn't. He eased the door open a little at a time until they had a good view of the dimly lighted room. The veiled woman was at a small organ playing it while Quentin, in a dark robe, stood at the altar behind the table with the grinning skull. He was staring upwards and murmuring some unintelligible words to the accompaniment of the music. There were a half-dozen young women in similar black robes kneeling before him in a line, their heads bowed.

It sickened her to see this weird gathering. Old Jasper had been right in saying that Quentin looked pale. He surely did. He ended his incantation and stared down the room at them. Seeing them in the open doorway he left the altar and strode down to challenge them.

"Neither of you believe," he said angrily. "Why have you intruded here?"

"Who knows. We might become devotees of your cult," Barnabas said mockingly. "You should welcome us."

"I know where you stand," Quentin told him, the nerve in his cheek twitching.

In the background the woman wearing the veil continued to play on the organ in a mournful fashion. The others remained kneeling and seemingly not knowing there had been an intrusion of the ritual in the softly lighted room. Anita became aware of a sweet-smelling incense filling the air. It made her feel slightly nauseated. She began to wish they would soon leave.

"You have been most anxious to welcome this young woman to your group," Barnabas said, indicating her.

"That is none of your affair," Quentin said sharply.

"I hear you were out this evening," Barnabas said. "You may be interested in hearing that it has been a night for phantoms. First, Miss Burgess saw the ghost of your friend Mara and then she was attacked by the werewolf."

Quentin showed uneasiness. "I must go back to the ritual."

"Strange you didn't encounter the phantoms?" Barnabas said.

"I have no more time to give you," Quentin said, his hand on the door as he made ready to close it.

Barnabas gazed around the black-draped room. "It is not as ornate as your headquarters in Venice was. But then you haven't nearly as many adherents as you had there."

"Good night," Quentin said firmly.

"Keep your eyes open for the werewolf," Barnabas said in his mocking fashion as they left the room. "It could be that you might summon him through your black mass. They claim werewolves respond to such incantations." Quentin showed them a white, angry face as he closed the door on them. They heard a latch click on the other side of the door while they stood there in the dark hall. Evidence that they would not be allowed to easily enter the forbidden room again.

They went back downstairs with the macabre organ music trailing after them. In the reception hall they found old Jasper Collins leaning on his cane waiting for them. "What was going on up there?" he wanted to know.

"Quentin was leading his ladies in an incantation to the Devil," Barnabas said with a grim smile.

The old man frowned. "Was my Georgina there?"

"I'm afraid so."

"I don't want her mixed up in such things," Jasper said angrily, thumping his cane tip on the floor. "That Quentin is a scoundrel."

"You must be patient," Barnabas said.

"Patient!" the old man echoed scornfully. "You could put a stop to all this if you wanted to. You have powers as strong as his!"

Barnabas showed a quizzical expression. "I wonder."

"Of course you have," Jasper Collins said indignantly. "If that young lady wasn't here I'd speak more freely. But you know what I mean."

"I have an idea," Barnabas said. "And I still advise patience."

They left the old man sputtering in the doorway of the mansion as they stepped out into the foggy night again. Barnabas placed a protective arm around her as they walked back towards the cottage.

She said, "It's a shame to have that old man feeling so badly."

"He's worried about Georgina and with cause."

"He seemed very sure you could do something. If you can, why don't you?"

Barnabas's smile was sad. "Jasper is old and senile. He has all sorts of fanciful notions. That among them."

"But he must have some basis for saying what he did," she persisted.

"I'm going to ask you to have faith in me," Barnabas told her. "And I don't want any more questions."

"Very well," she said quietly.

She was hurt by his refusal to take her further into his confidence. She had the impression that he possessed strong powers which he would not reveal. And old Jasper and others appeared to have the same idea. They felt he was able to challenge and defeat Quentin if and when he wished. So why was he holding back this way?

He said, "Any one of those girls kneeling before that altar could have been the one masquerading as Mara's ghost tonight."

"Why not the woman in the veil at the organ?" she asked. "I believe that is Mara."

"Possibly," he said. "I have a plan for finding out. I'll talk to you about it later."

"I don't see that we accomplished much in our call on Quentin," she said with some bitterness.

"You are wrong in that," he assured her. "I found out exactly what I wanted to."

Now they were close to the cottage and Barnabas halted. "I won't go in again. It would only lead to a long and pointless discussion with your brother. Like you and Jasper he would expect an instant solution for all this from me. And I can't offer it."

She looked up at him with a rueful smile. "You're a very strange man."

"And you're a most lovely young woman," he said in his low, charming voice. And with that he drew her to him and kissed her.

The kiss brought a look of surprise to her pretty face. When he let her go, she said, "What makes your lips so cold?"

"A long-time affliction," he said. "I've gotten accustomed to it."

"When will you see us again?"

"Tomorrow evening, I promise," he said. "And don't be uneasy if I'm late. You mustn't ever go out in search of me after darkness falls. The grounds are not safe."

"I'll remember," she said.

"Now go inside," he said with another of his warm smiles. "I'll wait until you've closed the door behind you."

She left him with reluctance. When she entered the cottage she found it quiet. The stillness in the air bothered her. There was no sign of her brother so she decided he must have gone to bed, having wearied of waiting for her. She waited a few moments and then went to the door of his bedroom and knocked on it.

"Jeffrey! Are you in there?" she asked.

There was no reply. So she knocked again and called his name. There was still no reply. Now she began to have a growing sensation of fear. There was something awesome and weird in the strange quiet. She tried the knob of the door and found it turned easily. Now she opened it and went inside. The bed was empty and there was no one in the shadowed room.

She backed out into the hallway, alarmed. Quickly she made a search of all the rest of the house. Jeffrey simply wasn't there. He had apparently gone out somewhere during her absence. She couldn't believe he would be so foolhardy after the experience of the early evening. She didn't know what to do.

Going to the front door she opened it cautiously and stared out into the darkness. Then she quickly closed it and latched it. Memories of the hideous face of the ghost and the snarling werewolf came back to make her tremble. She had no choice but to wait up for Jeffrey's return and let him in.

The fire in the fireplace had almost gone out and she was becoming dreadfully sleepy. The room was getting cold so she lifted two medium sized pieces of wood from the stack beside the fireplace and put them on the burning embers. Then she used the poker to settle them in and get them in a position to burn.

When she had seen this task completed she sat down in one of the comfortable chairs before the fireplace and stared into the flames. Where could Jeffrey have gone? Why hadn't he waited for her return? Had the ghost of the sinister Mara come as Barnabas predicted she might. And lured him out into the thick fog and blackness?

Had he also seen that terribly disfigured face and the shock of it had sent him stumbling off into the night? The legend of the Gorgon's face claimed that she could even strike men dead with her ugliness. Anita frowned at giving such thoughts credence. She must fight off her growing panic. No doubt Jeffrey had followed them over to the main house. And he might have met Barnabas on his way back and stopped to talk with him.

This comforted her so much that she relaxed and dropped off to sleep. When she opened her eyes it was much later, for the logs in the fireplace had burned out and there were only embers again. She glanced at the wall clock and saw that it was after four in the morning. This completely shocked her. She jumped to her feet and went to the door fearing that Jeffrey might have returned and she'd been sleeping too deeply to hear him and let him in.

Now she rebuilt the fire and began pacing nervously, not daring to sit down for fear she would fall asleep. She kept moving about and hoping Jeffrey would return until dawn showed in the sky. The fog was still thick but daylight was forcing its way on the morning.

Nine o'clock came and there was no sign of Jeffrey coming back. Now she knew something must be wrong. She dared not guess what might have happened. She tried to take some breakfast and managed to swallow only a scrap of toast and drink a little tea.

It was about nine thirty on the gray morning that she heard the carriage come up to the door and halt. She rushed to open the door and it was David Benson in raincoat and hat. The young man came into the living room of the cottage and removing his hat looked at her with a troubled expression on his youthful face.

"I guess you wonder why I'm here so early in the day," he said.

Panic was in her eyes. "It's about Jeffrey?"

"About Jeffrey?"

"Yes. My brother! He's been missing since last night. I'm almost frantic with worry!"

"I'm sorry," he said.

She looked at him with dismay. "Then you haven't come with word of him?"

"I'm afraid not."

"What is it?" She felt he might know something and be afraid to tell her.

The young man swallowed hard. "I shouldn't worry you when you are so upset already."

"Please go on!" she begged.

"I came to warn you that the werewolf showed itself on the edge of the village last night."

She nodded. "I saw it."

His eyes widened. "Here?"

"Yes. Where else was it seen?"

David Benson looked grave. "Some of the village men saw it jumping over the picket fence of a farmhouse on the upper end of the village. The house in which that maid lived who Quentin Collins discharged. The one who spread the scandal about his black magic activities."

"Go on," she said faintly.

David frowned. "I'd better wait."

"Please!"

"Well, the girl had been in the farmhouse alone. They went in to see if she was all right. And they found her dead on the kitchen floor. Her throat ripped open!"

"Oh, no!" she said in horror.

David Benson nodded grimly. "The villagers think Quentin decided to silence her. And I guess perhaps they are right. I think some of them are planning to come out here for a showdown. There are murmurings of wanting to put the torch to Collinwood and drive him away from the area."

"So it has come to that," she said in a small voice.

"I wanted to warn you and your brother there could be violence tonight and you'd better get away from here."

She shook her head in a dazed fashion. "I don't know what to say or do. I can't decide on anything without Jeffrey."

The young man sighed. "I know how you must feel. Have you any idea where he might have gone? I'll stay with you until you have some word of him. If I had some idea of where he might have gone

I'd make a search for him."

"It's hard to say," she murmured. "So many things happened last night." She went on to tell him about Mara's ghost and the werewolf, and of the visit she and Barnabas paid Quentin later.

"No wonder Quentin looked pale," David said with disgust. "He'd just returned from committing a murder."

She closed her eyes. "It's too horrible!"

"I'd better start trying to locate Jeffrey," he said. "I could begin by checking at Collinwood and the barns. Someone there may have seen him."

"I suppose you have to begin somewhere."

He started for the door, then paused. "Should I go to the old house and let Barnabas know?"

"Not yet. Not until the evening. He never leaves the house in the daytime."

David frowned. "Surely in an emergency like this?"

"Not yet," she said. "Don't bother him yet."

David opened the door to go out but then stopped where he stood, for the venerable Jasper Collins was framed there in the doorway with an expression on his gnarled face that could only spell bad news.

Leaning heavily on his cane, the old man limped into the room and reached out to pat her arm. "You must have courage," he said. "There has been a bad accident. Your brother is dead."

CHAPTER 12

The shock of the old man's words coming on top of her already shattered state made her behave in an unusual way. She was temporarily numbed to the announcement of Jeffrey's death so that she took it in a matter-of-fact fashion. Staring with dulled eyes, she tried to collect her thoughts.

"How?" she managed.

"The cliffs," Jasper Collins said. "One of the stableboys found him on the beach. He must have lost his way in the fog and stumbled over."

"No," she said in a whisper. "No. It was murder."

The old man looked embarrassed. "I don't know anything about that," he said. "I just know they found him there and he was killed by the fall."

David Benson asked, "Did they move the body?"

"They're doing that now," Jasper said. "I guess they're taking it to Collinwood to wait on this young lady's orders. They thought that would be best."

"They?" she questioned sharply.

The old man lowered his eyes. "Quentin."

"So Quentin is taking full charge," she said bitterly. "How kind of him after arranging Jeffrey's death in the first place!"

"I'd be careful what you said to him," the old man warned

her. "At least until you have Barnabas around to back you."

She was beginning to think she would faint. "Barnabas hasn't done anything."

"He will," Jasper said. "You wait."

David Benson had an arm around her. "You'd better take a rest for a little," he said.

"I'll be all right," she protested. But she let him guide her to an easy chair and seat her in it.

David hovered over her, his young face shadowed with concern. "Are you going to be all right?" he asked.

"Yes, of course," she said.

Old Jasper limped over and leaning on his cane said, "I'll have Georgina come to stay with you."

"No," she said, sitting up straight. "None of them! None of Quentin's circle."

"You can't be here alone," the old man worried.

"I want to," she said. "At least for a little."

David Benson turned to Jasper. "Can you stay here for a while? Until I make some inquiries for her?"

"Yes. I'd be glad to," Jasper said. "That is, if she wants me to."

She slumped back in the chair and shut her eyes. "Yes. I would like that. Someone I can trust." And almost at once she fell into an exhausted sleep.

When she awoke, Jasper was sitting in a chair near her leaning on his cane and looking like some ancient figure carved out of wood. He eyed her with concern.

"You feel better?"

"I suppose so," she said.

"You only slept for a little."

"It was enough."

The old man sighed. "You should get away from here. You should let him drive you back to Collinsport and leave as soon as you can."

She was staring straight ahead, much more assured now. Her mind made up. "No," she said. "I'll remain and settle what Jeffrey came here to do."

"You can't fight Quentin," the old man said. "He's in league with the Devil."

"Then he doesn't have too dependable an accomplice," she observed quietly.

The old man looked unhappy. "He'll get around you now that you haven't your brother to depend on. You'll wind up like my daughter and Laura Cranston and the rest! You'll be his slave!"

"No," she said, looking at him very directly. "You mustn't worry about that."

"I will," the old man promised. "That girl was murdered in the village last night. And your brother eliminated as well. Things are going Quentin's way and nothin' will stop him."

She said, "Barnabas can."

"Maybe," Jasper said. "I believed it up until now. But I'm starting to wonder."

Their conversation was interrupted by David Benson's return. He came in and sat down next to her to tell her the details of the finding of Jeffrey's body and what had been done.

Sighing, he said, "It could have been an accident. Quentin Collins makes it seem that it was. He even pointed out a depression in the path where your brother could have lost his footing in the fog."

"I'm sure he made it seem logical," she said with irony.

"I know how you feel," David said. "But you shouldn't rush to conclusions."

"Where is my brother?"

"At Collinwood. They've sent for a casket. You can go and see him any time you like."

She rose from the chair in a kind of dazed fashion. "I would like to go now," she announced.

The three of them rode over to Collinwood in the carriage. None of them spoke during the short ride. When they reached the imposing mansion Quentin was at the door to greet them. He looked pale and there were deep lines of weariness on his face.

He said, "You must know how painful this is for me. You have my deepest sympathy."

She avoided looking at him. "Where is Jeffrey?"

"I'll take you to him," he said.

He led her into the living room where her brother's body was temporarily resting on a chaise lounge until the undertaker arrived. She looked down at his strained face and the anguish she saw there made her own eyes fill with tears. Jeffrey had not died peacefully. His face showed that.

David, at her side, touched her arm to give her support. She gazed at the beloved, pale face so rigid in death and then turned away. Then at the doorway she was met by Georgina and Laura Cranston. Both women looked white-faced and distraught.

Georgina said, "If there's anything we can do?"

Laura nodded. "Can we go back to the cottage with you?"

"Perhaps you would like to stay here with us," Georgina suggested.

Anita shook her head to their suggestions and walked on by them. She was wondering where the woman in black with the veil was. It was strange she wasn't there also to offer her sympathies. But then she never spoke.

Quentin came close to her and spoke urgently in her ear. "I must speak to you alone for a moment before you leave."

She gave him a stony look. Then she followed him down the hallway to the library. He waited for her to enter first and then he came in and shut the door so they would not be overheard.

He came to her tensely. "You mustn't blame me for this."

She looked at him with derision. "Of course. You're always blameless."

"They are spreading poisonous gossip about me. But I count on you not to believe any of it."

"Strange that the same thing happened in Venice until you had to leave there," she said scathingly.

"I'll not be driven from Collinwood," he said with a hint of returning anger.

"That will be interesting to see," she said.

"I don't want to talk about that," he said. "I want to tell you about Jeffrey's death."

"Oh?" She raised her eyebrows. "So you admit knowing about it."

He looked unhappy. "I had to say that he fell to his death by accident, but we both know that wasn't what happened."

She stared at him. "Your frankness shocks me."

"Hear me out," he pleaded. "I'm positive it was Mara's ghost that led him out into the night and to his death."

"I thought you might say that."

"I believe it to be true. When he saw her face, the ugliness of that Gorgon mask, he could not bear it. And he toppled back over the cliff to his death!"

"And that is your answer to what happened?"

"Yes." Quentin studied her anxiously.

"I'll have to think about it," she said.

"I'm positive it was the ghost that was responsible," he said.

"Thank you for telling me."

"Won't you stay here?"

"No. I'm returning to the cottage and packing. I'll be leaving tonight or first thing in the morning."

Quentin frowned. "I think you should reconsider. Move here in the main house. We'd all be glad to have you."

"Thank you," she said. "David will be waiting."

Quentin frowned. "Who is this David Benson?"

"A lawyer from Boston. He is home on holiday. He claims to know you slightly."

"I don't recall him," Quentin said.

"It's of no importance," she told him. "I'll want Jeffrey's body transferred to the night boat when I leave. I'll see to his burial in Philadelphia."

"Of course," Quentin said. "Though again I think he would be as happy buried here in the Collins cemetery. And you could remain and recover from your tragic loss."

She eyed him coldly. "How kind you are!"

He was not unaware of the irony of her tone. With a shamed look he opened the door for her and escorted her back to a waiting David. The fog lay like a gray mantle over the countryside as the young man drove her back to the cottage. The bleak day matched her mood.

When they were in the living room of the cottage, the young man asked her, "What next?"

"I'll pack and leave in the morning."

"Why not tonight? I warned you there could be violence here. The villagers are in an ugly mood."

She gave him a knowing glance. "I can't leave without seeing Barnabas," she said.

"You're not taking up your brother's mad battle for revenge?"

"I will count on Barnabas to act for me. I'm sure he can be trusted to do so," she said. "I'll not go without first talking with him."

The young man frowned. "But he's such an eccentric! Not leaving the house on a day filled with turmoil like this! How can you know that he'll show up here tonight?"

"He will come," she said confidently. "His servant will tell him what has happened and he will be here as soon as dusk shows."

David Benson continued to look worried. "I'll have to return to the village," he said. "And I don't like the idea of leaving you alone here."

"I'll be perfectly all right," she said. "And Barnabas will protect me through the night."

"If you're sure."

"I am sure."

The young man took a deep breath. "I'll still think about you," he said. "And I'll come in the carriage to get you and your baggage first thing in the morning."

"That would be helpful," she said. "And thank you for all you've done so far."

"It hasn't been enough," he said. He touched his lips to her forehead in parting. She watched him drive off in the fog feeling a deep bond with him.

The day seemed interminably long. She kept busy with packing but several times as she came upon Jeffrey's things she thought she would break down. Evening finally came and she had some broth, toast and tea. And as soon as it was dusk there came a familiar knock on her door. Before she opened it she knew it had to be Barnabas.

He embraced her and held her close to him. In a gentle voice, he said, "You can't imagine the sadness and regret I felt on hearing about Jeffrey."

"You can't blame yourself," she said. "Coming here was his decision. And leaving here last night was his own idea. They somehow tricked him into it. Quentin declares that it was the ghost of Mara who was responsible."

The handsome face of Barnabas was grim. "That sounds like Quentin."

"What are we going to do? Or should we do anything? David Benson says the villagers are aroused because of the murder of that servant girl last night. Of course they think that Quentin did it in the form of the werewolf."

"Very likely that's true," Barnabas agreed.

"And some of the villagers are threatening to come here tonight and burn Collinwood down as well as killing Quentin."

Barnabas frowned. "I would hate to see Collinwood destroyed. And to have it happen because of the disgrace Quentin has brought upon the family."

"It may be impossible to stop them."

He sighed. "That is true."

"Have you any plan?"

"I'd like to set a trap for a ghost," he said. "But to do so you'll have to take the role of decoy."

"I'd be willing to."

"I've never doubted that," he said. "But should I ask you to?"

"I have to find out about that ghost," she said seriously. "In any case I don't know whether it is a ghost or Mara alive. When I was at Collinwood the woman in the veil didn't show herself."

"Maybe you'll see her tonight," Barnabas said quietly. "Do you feel you can stand the sight of that hideous face again?"

"Yes."

"Then in an hour or so I want you to leave the cottage by yourself and begin walking along the cliff path. I'll be waiting nearby but it's important that you seem to be alone. In that way I have an idea you will be visited again by Mara's ghost."

"As long as you're somewhere close," she said.

"I promise I will be," Barnabas told her.

So it was settled. He left her a short while after. She sat before the fireplace wondering what the night would bring, asking herself what terrors would be resolved and what mysteries explained.

Quentin had shadowed all their lives with his pact with evil. Arnold had lost his life because of it. And now it was Jeffrey. Whether Mara had been a victim of the Satanist circle or was still an active part of it might be decided within the hour.

If the phantom Mara with the hideous Gorgon's face responded to the trap Barnabas was setting for her, they might learn whether she was ghost or human. They might also discover whether the woman in the black veil was Mara in disguise.

At last it was time to go. She put on her cloak and went out into the chill fog. It was almost as nasty as the previous night. She walked swiftly across the wet lawn to the path that ran along the edge of the cliff. She was trembling slightly as she stood there for a moment high above the sound of the waves below. Somewhere out in the fog she heard the blast of a ship's horn. It was too early for the night boat so it had to be one of the many coastal freighters that served the various towns and villages.

Barnabas had promised to be somewhere near but there was no sign of him. She could only begin walking along the path and see what would happen. Perhaps the phantom would be wary and not show herself. She might be going through this ordeal for nothing.

The fog was heavier in some places than in others. At times it would block her vision for even a short distance and then it would clear a little. To the right she could see the glow of distant yellow squares marking the windows of Collinwood. She thought of how cold and motionless Jeffrey's body had been, Jeffrey, who would be resting in a coffin in the big mansion by now.

She was deep in those thoughts and hardly noticed the figure standing in the path before her until she was almost upon it. Then she halted and caught her breath. She knew only too well what would happen next. And it did! The phantom turned to reveal the shimmering white party dress with its wide flowing skirt and low cut bodice. And the face leering at her was the same horror as before!

Anita took a step back and raised her hands to screen the hideous features from her. "No!" she protested.

But the gargoyle with the twisted, nightmare face came steadily closer to her. A low chuckle escaped the distorted lips and a hand stretched out to grasp her! She screamed and was about to turn and try to escape the monster.

It was at that moment Barnabas emerged from the darkness and fog to spring on the phantom. A cry of alarm escaped the figure in the white dress as she struggled to escape his grasp. But Barnabas had superior strength and as Anita watched in awe she saw him overpower the strange creature and then reach up to that twisted face. With a deft movement he tore off a mask to reveal the features of Dorothy Carr!

Anita couldn't believe her eyes. But standing there with an abject expression was her friend from Venice. The daughter of the wealthy Alexander Carr at whose home she had first been introduced to Quentin. Dorothy who had pretended so well to be her friend right up to that last day they had met at St. Mark's Square!

"You!" she gasped.

"Yes," Dorothy said with just a hint of defiance. "You never guessed I was part of Quentin's cult! That I was more important to him than any of the others!"

"You kept the secret well!" Anita gasped. "So you were the veiled widow in black?"

The red-haired beauty looked at her sadly. "Yes. Quentin made me conceal my identity. He was afraid my father or some of my relatives in America might have hired a detective to try and trace where I had vanished. This way I wouldn't be recognized. Of course when you and Jeffrey arrived I had a double reason for the disguise. But I didn't kill Arnold. It was Mara who did that. And then because she was jealous of me and threatened to tell the police about the black magic circle, Quentin finished her."

Anita asked, "Who killed Jeffrey?"

The other girl looked down. "I lured him out here. But Quentin sent him over the cliff to his death."

She'd barely finished speaking when they saw and heard the wagons rolling across the lawn of Collinwood. There were two of them, large wagons with lanterns mounted on them and filled with angry villagers. The noise of the rumbling wagons mixed with the ominous shouts of those crowded in the clumsy vehicles.

Dorothy stared at the wagons as they careened towards the mansion. Terror showed in her lovely face. "What now?" she demanded.

"The Collinsport people have finally lost patience," Barnabas said grimly. "It looks like the end of Collinwood and Quentin!"

"No!" The redhead cried. With an elusive movement she escaped from Barnabas and began racing towards the house.

Anita glanced at him. "What now?"

"Let her go," he said grimly. "We've found out all we need to know. She's only placing herself in danger." There were loud cries as the wagons drew up before Collinwood and angry men jumped out and approached the mansion. Almost at once several torches showed in the hands of the group. Dorothy had vanished somewhere in the darkness.

Barnabas told her, "You remain in the background. I have to take some part in this."

"No," she protested. "You'll be hurt!"

"I have no choice," he said. "I can't stand by and watch them burn Collinwood down."

With that he left her and made his way across the lawn to the entrance of the old mansion. She followed a little distance behind him and then came to a halt on the edge of the furious mob. The men in front were brandishing torches and threatening to burn the place down unless Quentin showed himself.

She saw Barnabas reach the house and mount the front steps. He shouted some placating words to the crowd and then went inside. The angry roar from the sullen mob grew in strength and they surged towards the entrance, a tide of wrathful humanity!

Now the door opened and Barnabas emerged with Quentin. He looked thoroughly frightened. Barnabas tried to address the angry group but could not make himself heard above their shouts of rage. They were ready to mount the steps and seize one or both of the Collins men. Anita was in a state of panic for the safety of Barnabas.

While she watched with bated breath a completely unexpected thing happened. One moment it was Quentin standing with Barnabas and the next it was a greenish-gray, snarling wolf! The instantaneous transformation brought a momentary hush to the mob.

The great animal with burning amber eyes took advantage of this instant of shock to bound from the steps and cut through the crowd. The angry men drew back to let it pass, still shaken by what they had seen. Then as the supernatural monster bounded towards the cliffs the figure of Dorothy emerged from the shadows to run after it, screaming out for it to wait for her.

Her appearance and screams seemed to rouse the mob from its state of shock. The tide of irate townspeople flowed after the escaping werewolf and the girl. Across the foggy darkness they pursued the two with lighted torches high and shouts of rage. Shots were fired in a veritable barrage. One of them caught Dorothy and she paused in her flight, arms thrown upward and then collapsed face down in the grass.

The werewolf bounded on. The shots continued and again one found its mark. The greenish-gray monster came to a quivering pause for a moment and Anita was sure it had been hit in a vital place. But after a fleeting second it raced on to the edge of the cliff and vanished. The crowd gathered on the brink of the cliff.

Anita was standing watching the eerie drama when Barnabas joined her. "That rids Collinwood of Quentin," he said. "Dorothy is dead and he's somewhere down there."

She looked at him fearfully. "Surely he must be dead."

Barnabas gave her a meaningful glance. "I wouldn't count on that. He does have supernatural powers, you'll remember. But he'll stay away for a time at least."

She eyed the crowd. "What about Collinwood?"

"It will be safe now. They've rid themselves of Quentin and the werewolf threat."

The prediction Barnabas made was correct. The crowd dispersed quietly. She and Barnabas returned to Collinwood where the elderly Jasper had taken charge. A subdued Georgina served them a warm drink as they planned for the future.

Barnabas told the old man, "I'll be leaving on the night boat tomorrow night. I assume Georgina will come into the estate."

"She was the next named in the will," Jasper said with satisfaction. "She'll do well enough now that she is free of Quentin."

"I'll be leaving along with you," Anita told Barnabas. And to Jasper, she said, "I'd like you to have my brother's coffin sent to the boat."

"I'll gladly take care of that," the old man said. "I only wish you both would stay here a little longer."

But they both were anxious to leave the turmoil of Collinwood. It might be some time before things were back in smooth order there. David Benson came to help her with her final packing and transferring her luggage to the village. Barnabas had told her they would meet on the night boat as he did not expect to go to the docks until after dark.

David surprised her by telling her that he had decided to take the same boat back to Boston. "I want to make the trip with you," he said. "I'd be leaving in a few days in any case."

Seated beside him in the carriage she reached over and touched the hand in which he held the reins. "I have never had a better friend than you," she said softly.

David glanced at her. "Mightn't I hope to be more than a friend one day?"

Her eyes were sad. "I can't talk about that now," she said, and turned her head.

"It is Barnabas, isn't it?" David said in a kind voice. "You're in love with him." She didn't deny it.

The night boat arrived promptly on time and she and David boarded it. She was upset because she had not seen a sign of Barnabas or his servant. After a short wait at the wharf for loading the ship moved out into the waters of the bay again. She stood at the railing watching the faint lights of the village vanish in the distance and thinking of the first time she had seen them. So much had happened since.

David was at her side. "I'm probably thinking the same thing you are. Of the night we arrived."

She turned to him in the darkness of the deck. "You're right.

I'm remembering it was the first time I ever saw Barnabas. He was standing a distance back in the shadows, apart from the rest of us, watching." She smiled forlornly. "Later he said something about it to me. That there were people doomed to always remain aloof in the shadows."

David Benson said, "Barnabas is a fine man."

"I wonder where he is," she worried. "He promised he would leave tonight. That we would go to Boston together."

David said gently, "He's not on board. And he asked me to give you a message. But not until the boat had left the wharf."

Anita felt a tightening around her heart. She searched the face of the young man at her side. "What did he ask you to tell me?"

"To forget Collinwood and all its people," David said. "To look for the happiness he wishes you elsewhere."

She said nothing, turning to stare at the shore with eyes brimming with tears. There was nothing but darkness. Collinsport had vanished in the night.

BOOK TWENTY-ONE

Barnabas, Quentin and the Haunted Cave

Coming Soon

**WILL THE EVIL FORCES AT COLLINWOOD DESTROY
BARNABAS COLLINS, TOO?**

Harriet Turnbridge fears for her life as, one by one, the members of
her family are brutally murdered. She turns to Barnabas Collins for
help.

Barnabas and Harriet are close on the trail of the killer when they are
tricked into following him into a secret cave far beneath Collinwood.
Almost immediately, the only entrance is sealed off, and Barnabas
and Harriet are trapped in this grotesque world of ghost-like
stalactites and treacherous, bottomless black pools.

Will Harriet and Barnabas meet the phantom murderer in this
horrible realm of the dead? Or will they escape to face an even
deadlier enemy?

ᴅARK ꙅHADOWS

Published by **Hermes** Press

COMING SOON FROM
HERMES PRESS

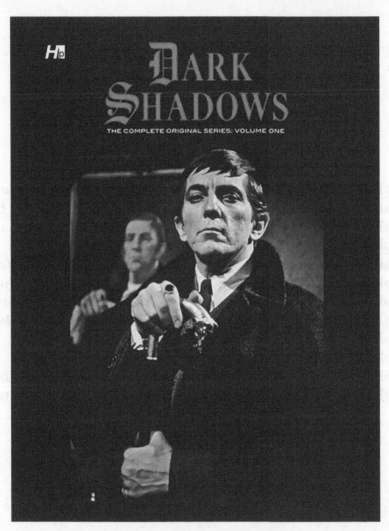

DARK SHADOWS

Published by **Hermes** Press

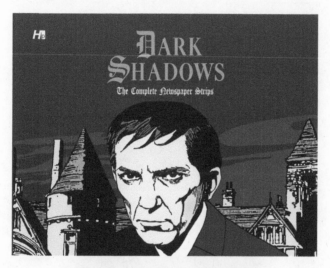

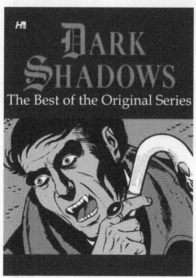

Visit **www.hermespress.com** to learn more
and see additional *Dark Shadows* titles.